STOLEN RING TIME

YAN KALANDAROV

CONTENTS

Chapter 1   1
Chapter 2   15
Chapter 3   31
Chapter 4   41
Chapter 5   57
Chapter 6   67
Chapter 7   81
Chapter 8   93
Chapter 9   115
Chapter 10   131
Chapter 11   151
Chapter 12   161
Chapter 13   175
Chapter 14   191
Chapter 15   205

From the Author   209

ONE

R ussel was never one to look for trouble of any kind. He never
    wanted to be the center of attention and avoided confrontation
where he could.

Unfortunately for him, trouble was on his tail, and it came in the
form of two varsity football players.

"Where are you in such a rush to? Pretty boy!" Adam called out as
he and his pal Randy picked up the pace.

Russel didn't say anything and kept walking down the hallway,
hoping to spot a teacher, a counselor, or any adult who would deter
Adam and Randy from harassing him.

He turned a corner and only spotted Kyle, who he had never
spoken to, approaching his locker at the other end of the hall.

Kyle was fiddling with his locker when out of the corner of his eye,
he saw Russel Coleman shuffling down the hall nervously, hunched
over with hands in his pockets and his uneven curly bangs in his face.
He was being trailed by Randy and Adam, which explained his
distressed demeanor.

Kyle entered his lock combination instinctively while keeping an
eye on the other end of the hall. He was dripping with sweat after an
intense workout at the High School gym. His shoulder and quads were

on fire, and opening up his locker seemed like a tall task. It had to be done. He couldn't go home in his sweaty gym clothes, or he'd never hear the end of it from his mother. Deep down, he knew she meant well; besides, he couldn't afford to get sick before the weekend.

Kyle had a big show coming up. He was wrestling in the opening match of Brawlamania at the local YMCA. Three weeks away from his eighteenth birthday, he was the youngest person on the card that night, and he was determined not to let that stop him from stealing the show.

Most of his high school peers were still trying to figure out who they wanted to be when they grew up, but Kyle knew exactly what he wanted. He had a big dream of being a professional wrestler, and he wasn't waiting to graduate from high school that summer before pursuing it. He started lifting weights religiously to fill out what was a slender frame only a year ago, and he grew out his dark brown hair to the point where it would rub against the peach fuzz on his jaw.

By the time Kyle pulled a dry T-shirt over his head, Russel was close enough for him to see the panic on his face.

"Hey, rich boy! Where are you off to in such a hurry?" Adam asked as he and Randy picked up the pace.

Kyle stuffed the sweaty clothes into his backpack while keeping his eyes fixed on what was happening only a few feet away.

"Hey! We are talking to you!" Randy exclaimed.

They caught up to Russel, and Adam grabbed him by the strap on his bookbag and jerked it back sending Russel tumbling backwards until he crashed into one of the lockers and slid down to the floor.

"When the co-captains of the football team address you, you show them some respect!" Randy said. He and Adam stood over Russel, whose eyes darted from one person to the other.

Kyle brushed his hair away from his face and slammed his locker shut. "I didn't know picking on the new kid was a football drill."

Adam and Randy both shifted their attention to Kyle from across the hall giving Russel a chance to stand up. They looked at each other with identical smirks on their faces.

"Kyle, we know you play fight on the weekends, but I'll be glad to give you a real beat down if that's what you're looking for," Adam said.

"Did you say *I* as in you're going do something without Randy jumping in?" Kyle asked. He placed his backpack on the floor next to his locker and realized he wasn't feeling the after effects of the work out anymore. "I don't think you've ever been able to give anyone a beat down without a few of your jock buddies jumping in."

"You watch your filthy mouth, Kyle!" Adam shouted. His eyes wide with rage as he stomped towards Kyle.

Russel was frozen in place while Randy stood back, cracking his knuckles.

"Stay out of this!" Adam ordered.

Kyle took a deep breath and brushed his hair back just in time to see Adam lunge at him. He ducked under and spun around quick enough to wrap his arms around Adam's head and neck, putting him into a sleeper hold.

"You're going to pay for this!" Adam whispered. His arms were flailing wildly, but he was nowhere close to freeing himself from Kyle's grasp.

The flailing started to get progressively slower, at which point Kyle let go and shoved Adam forward and away from himself.

Adam landed on all fours and was coughing up a lung. "This isn't over!" He whispered as loudly as he could. He forced himself up, stumbled towards Randy, and motioned for the two of them to go.

Russel remained motionless against the lockers.

"Are you alright over here?" Kyle asked. He walked towards Russel.

"I am," Russel said, nodding his head. "Thanks for doing that."

"It's no big deal," Kyle said and started walking towards the exit. "You should probably get out of here. There is a good chance they'll be back with their buddies."

Russel stood up and followed after Kyle. "I'm Russel, by the way." He extended his hand for a handshake,

Kyle shook it reluctantly without slowing down. "I know who you are."

"Thanks for helping me out over there," Russel said.

"Don't get used to it. Judging by your handshake, you're in good enough shape to stand up for yourself," Kyle said and shook his head.

"I know," Russell replied. "I didn't catch your name."

"Kyle Trevor."

"Nice to meet you, Kyle."

"My car is this way," Kyle said as he swung open the exit door. "You don't have to keep following me. I won't tell your girlfriend about what happened."

"My girlfriend?" Russel let out a nervous laugh. "I'm not worried about that since I don't have one anymore."

Kyle raised an eyebrow, expressing interest in this conversation for the first time. "I thought you were with Chelsea. She snatched you up on the first day of school, didn't she?"

"Yes. That was done right after the holidays."

"Keeping up with the gossip is not at the top of my list. You're probably better off."

"Perhaps I am," Russell said. "Those guys were after me because they wanted intimate details about Chelsea. Once I refused to share, they got aggressive with me."

"Refused to share, huh?" Kyle said and shook his head. "That automatically makes you the most decent guy Chelsea ever dated."

"Has she dated that many guys?"

"You're asking the wrong person. As I said, I don't keep up with the gossip," Kyle said and started walking away. "I have to get going. Stay out of trouble, Russel."

"There has to be something I can do to repay you," Russell said.

Kyle stopped and let out a visible sigh. He took his backpack off, reached in, and grabbed a piece of paper just as Russel caught up to him. "Here, take this."

"A flier?" Russel asked before he could read it.

"It's for a wrestling show that I'll be at. If you buy a ticket and tell them I told you about it, we'll call it even."

"Okay, sure," Russel said. "Tonight, at eight. I'll be there!"

Kyle climbed into his car and started it up.

He was certain that he wouldn't see Russel at the show and would probably never speak with him again.

———

Russel clicked the remote to open the garage door and pulled his Mustang convertible inside. Almost any other kid his age would love to have the car, but not Russel. He didn't like being the center of attention, but that's exactly what he was when he pulled into the parking lot on the first day of school. That was how he caught Chelsea Breen's attention and shot right up to the very top of the food chain in Reign Central High School.

He didn't last there very long. It wasn't his scene, and he was never able to make close connections with anyone in Chelsea's group of friends. He barely knew her, and they had been dating for almost four months.

Russel played the part Chelsea cast him in, but that was the root of the problem. He couldn't be himself, and it became more and more difficult to hide with each passing day. A few weeks in he made the mistake of opening up to Chelsea about how uncomfortable he felt. She pretended to understand just long enough to make it through the holiday season, where all of her friends and their boyfriends got together for Friendsgiving and then Christmas. Everyone had to take a couple's picture and post it all over social media to wish everyone Merry Christmas.

Once the holiday season was over Chelsea promptly broke up with Russel.

It seemed like a win for both of them at the time. Russel could be himself, and with Valentine's Day around the corner, Chelsea didn't miss a beat, as the potential suitors lined up as soon as the two of them broke up.

Russel became invisible to everyone in Chelsea's circle, and since he had never made any friends of his own, he was stuck being a loner for the better part of two months. Things only got worse once Chelsea spread a few nasty rumors about him, which automatically made him a target for those wishing to get Chelsea's attention.

Russel had no doubt that if Kyle hadn't stepped in, Adam and Randy would have recorded a video of him crawling on the floor, trying to regain his balance or perhaps something even worse.

"Russel! Do you plan on coming upstairs tonight?"

"I'm coming up," Russel said just loud enough for his Dad to hear.

He climbed out of the car, grabbed his bookbag, and made his way up the somewhat narrow spiral staircase.

"How was your day, son?" Felix asked, briefly glancing over at his son before putting the finishing touches on his tie.

"It was alright," Russel replied, unable to muster up much enthusiasm.

His father was the exact opposite of his disheveled son. Felix Coleman was in peak physical condition for a man in his mid-forties. There was not a hair out of place on either his head or his salt and pepper goatee. His suit was perfectly tailored, and his shoes were spotless. "What do you think?"

"You look great, Dad. What's the occasion tonight?" Russel asked in an attempt to steer the conversation away from school.

"I've got a few investors from China who couldn't wait until tomorrow to see the company's presentation about our newest product."

"Which is what exactly?" Russel asked and plopped down on the cushy chair across from where his Dad was getting ready.

"It's a new formula that will be used on violent criminals," Felix said. "One dose and they'll be docile, but functioning members of society."

"Is that even legal?"

"Not in the United States, but they are a little less strict about these things on the other side of the world," Felix said and made his way towards the same door that Russel used earlier. "Marlene made dinner before I sent her home for the weekend. Depending on how the meeting goes, I should be home no later than midnight."

"Good luck Dad," Russel said, forcing a smile that did not reach his eyes.

He warmed up the spaghetti and meatballs that were left behind by their housekeeper and walked down to the head of the long marble dinner table in the dining room.

Russel felt something bending in his pocket as he planted himself in the cushy chair. He reached into his pocket and pulled out the flier for Kyle's show.

He looked at the flier and then at the clock on the wall.

Oh, that's right! The show is tonight! He thought to himself. *It's at eight, I have to hurry.*

Russel scarfed down the food as quickly as he could, sucked down a glass of water and ran back down to the garage.

————

Russel pulled up to the YMCA and quickly realized he was not prepared for the cast of characters who were outside selling everything from T-shirts to headbands and action figures. There were men and women of all shapes and sizes. There was a variety of unique attires, hair styles, and even a few people with face paint.

Russel parked his car around the block and sat there for a minute, wondering if he was making a mistake. He ultimately decided that he owed it to Kyle to check out the show after what he did for him earlier.

He took a deep breath and started to walk towards the rowdy crowd that was gathering outside of the YMCA. He stuffed his hands into his pockets, admiring the people who were piling into what seemed to be a small middle school gym. He followed the flow of the crowd, which led towards the entrance.

He was greeted by a burly man with a messy beard and scraggly long hair at the door. "You've got a ticket? Otherwise, it's twenty bucks for general admission, forty for the front row."

"I'll take the twenty-dollar ticket," Russel said, reached into his front pocket and pulled out a twenty-dollar bill. "Kyle Trevor invited me to this show."

"Would you look at that? Kyle finally started to self-promote," the man said and laughed to himself. "About freaking time. You know what? We got a few seats open in the front row. Go straight down there and grab a seat. Enjoy the show!"

Russel was about to thank the guy, but he had already moved on to the next person in line. He made his way inside and it quickly became apparent that there was no air conditioning and minimal ventilation. The building was filling up quickly, with dozens of people still waiting outside.

There was even less order inside the building, as there were about twenty uneven rows or folding chairs leading up to the center where the ring was on a slightly elevated platform.

Russel followed the directions from the man at the door, but then realized that the ticket had no seat number.

Great, he thought to himself. *I should have stayed home.*

He glanced back at the entrance. People were squeezing through at an alarming rate. There was no way Russel could try to escape through there. Just as he was about to start the trek towards the front, he spotted Kyle setting up the ring. He was wearing bright blue tights, a sleeveless black shirt with what could only be a spray-painted version of his own face, and his hair was gelled back. Russel reluctantly pushed his way through the crowd until he was no longer at shouting distance.

"Hey! Kyle?" Russel said. He still wasn't completely sure if this was the same person who gave him the flier.

Kyle turned around. "You actually made it."

"I said I would, so here I am."

"Okay, grab a seat."

"Any seat?"

"Yeah, we are not doing assigned seats tonight," Kyle said as he secured the ring apron.

Russel sat down on the chair closet to him. "I guess good luck out there tonight?"

"Thanks," Kyle said dismissively.

Russel took the hint and did not force further conversation. He sat down and touched the metal barricade, which was the only thing between himself and the ring.

"Russel, judging by the look on your face, you've never been to a wrestling show like this before," Kyle said. "I'll be diving through the ropes about five minutes into my match, and there is a good chance we'll land right where you're sitting. Just be alert."

"Sure, I'll be alert," Russel said, examining the ring while Kyle jumped over the rail and jogged back to get ready for his match. *There is no way he is jumping over that top rope. He's definitely messing with me.*

———

Felix Coleman weaved in and out of traffic with precision. He wasn't running late, but he also wasn't as early as he would have liked to be. He hit the Bluetooth button on the steering wheel. "Call Alex."

The phone barely started to ring when the young man answered the phone, "Good evening Mr. Coleman."

"Alex, is everything ready?"

"Yes, sir," the young man replied. He was doing his best not to sound nervous. "Mr. Okada is in the conference room, and he came alone."

"No assistants or business partners," Felix said, mostly to himself.

"No sir."

"I'll be there in five minutes. Getting off the highway now."

He hung up before Alex had a chance to respond. He needed some time to collect himself before this somewhat unexpected meeting.

To the best of Felix's recollection, Mr. Okada specialized in robotics. There were rumors floating around that he had split away from his China based business partners and started his own company. It still didn't explain why he wanted to have a private meeting with Felix, who dealt primarily in cutting edge pharmaceuticals.

With his exit off the expressway in sight, Felix shifted into the right lane and sped up the ramp. He zipped through the back streets that led to his office and had his car parked in his designated parking spot moments later.

"Mr. Okada is in conference room three," Alex held the door open as Felix rushed past him and up the flight of stairs. Even though it was a rather cool spring evening, there was visible sweat coming down through the part on the left side of Alex's hair. The sleeves on his shirt were rolled up, and his tie was a bit loose around his collar, but Felix was too focused on the meeting to comment on it.

Mr. Okada was standing by the window overlooking the town of Reign. His back turned to the entrance. He was dressed in a traditional black suit, with a matching tie to go against a perfectly ironed shirt. His jet black hair was neatly combed to the side. The only thing that gave away his age were the subtle wrinkles under his eyes.

"Mr. Okada," Felix said as he walked through the door and

extended his right hand for a hand shake. "I hadn't expected to see you back in the US until next quarter."

"Likewise, but this simply couldn't wait." Mr. Okada walked over and shook Felix's hand.

"Let's get to it then," Felix said and motioned for Mr. Okada to join him at the long conference table in the center of the room. "Can we get you anything to drink?"

"I'm fine. Thank you."

Felix shot a quick glance at Alex who was standing by the door with a clipboard clasped against his chest. He knew exactly what that look meant. He nodded and exited the room, closing the door behind him.

"What brings you here on such short notice?" Felix asked.

"Your new substance," Mr. Okada replied.

"It's still in the early testing stages. We haven't even gone to human trials yet."

"That's where I think our partnership can be mutually beneficial. I recently purchased a small prison town on the outskirts of Nagasaki. This place houses the worst members of our society. I would like to test out the effectiveness of your substance on them."

"I see," Felix said and leaned back in chair. "Now, I'm sure your prison has a well-trained security force, but there are certain measures that need to be in place just in case something goes wrong."

"My security force is unique to put simply," Mr. Okada said. "Let me show you."

Mr. Okada pulled out his phone. He placed it on the table and clicked a few buttons on his smart watch. The phone produced a 3D projection no more than a foot tall, showing a bald man dressed in plain navy uniform, running through an elaborate obstacle course with ease.

"This is very impressive," Felix admitted. He couldn't take his eyes off the man who was jumping over six-foot walls as if he was at a kid's playground.

"Here comes the best part," Mr. Okada said and smiled at his projection.

As the man came to the end of the obstacle course, he wasn't even out of breath. When he was greeted by similar looking men at the finish line.

Felix leaned in to get a closer look.

It didn't take him long to realize what Mr. Okada wanted him to see.

"They're all identical," Felix said, his eyes shifting between the projection and Mr. Okada. "I'm looking at twenty-five identical men."

"Not exactly men, Mr. Coleman. They're androids."

"Those are by far the most advanced androids I've ever seen," Felix admitted.

"I'm glad you like them," Mr. Okada said. He turned off the projection and pulled his phone off the table. "My goal is to have them serve as prison guards, but despite that impressive showing, there are still a few kinks to work out."

"That's why you need my substance. You want the prisoners as docile as possible until you perfect your creation."

"Precisely. So, what do you say Mr. Coleman?"

"I'll have to consider it," Felix said. "Forward your files over to me, and I'll have my team look over everything."

"That will suffice," Okada said and extended his hand as he stood up.

Felix shook Okada's hand and said, "I'll have a decision for you by the end of the week."

———

It didn't take five minutes for Russel to find out that Kyle wasn't joking about diving outside the ring. Russel was mesmerized by the athleticism displayed by both Kyle and his much larger and by the looks of it, much older opponent; Robert Crude.

Luckily for everyone involved, Russel had quick reflexes and jumped out of the way when Kyle flew over the top rope just as he had predicted. He managed to come in contact with his opponent, but then somehow landed on his feet. He brushed his hair back and continued the match.

Kyle and Robert traded moves for a few minutes. When it looked like Kyle was going to win, Robert surprised him with a roll-up pin and won the match. Not too familiar with the inner workings of professional wrestling, Russel did not realize that Robert was the heel, or the bad guy, while Kyle was the baby face, a good guy.

After briefly selling his unexpected loss by sitting in the corner of the ring with his hands on his head, Kyle rolled out from under the bottom rope and limped back to the locker room.

Russel found himself enjoying the show a lot more than he expected and decided to stick around until the end of the show. Following the main event, there was an announcement about next month's show, as well as, other shows in the area.

"So, I take it you liked the show?" Kyle, showered and in street clothes, asked just as Russel stood up to leave.

"I really did. How long have you been doing this?"

"I started training as soon as I turned sixteen, so about two years now," Kyle said. He motioned for the two of them to head for the exit.

"I don't know much about wrestling but you seemed to be holding your own out there," Russel said.

"Robert actually trained me," Kyle said, and waved to one of the other performers on the way out the door. "A lot of what we do in the ring has to do with how good the other person is. Robert and I have mutual trust so it makes working together a lot easier."

"I see. That makes sense," Russel said.

"Thanks for coming, man. I'm going to wait for one of the other guys to see if I can catch a ride home."

"You didn't drive here?"

"The promoter doesn't want us taking up spots in the parking lot," Kyle said. "And I didn't have time to come look for parking."

"I actually parked right around the corner. I can give you a ride home."

"Sure. If you don't mind."

They walked to Russel's car quietly. Kyle broke the silence as soon Russel hit the remote start. "A convertible? No wonder Chelsea was all over you."

Russel cracked a smile and shook his head. "You can put your bag in the trunk."

Kyle did and climbed into the passenger seat. He examined the interior with just as much admiration as the exterior.

"I'm going to sound like a spoiled rich kid," Russel admitted. "But my dad bought me this car."

"You don't give off a spoiled rich kid vibe," Kyle said. "Plus, your dad bringing his business here basically revitalized our little town of Reign."

"That's what he does everywhere he goes," Russel said. He pulled out of the lot and handed Kyle his phone. "Put in your address."

"You don't need the GPS. I know this town like the back of my hand," Kyle said and took hold of the phone only to put it down in the cup holder. "My mom's accounting business really picked up once your dad opened up his office and his factory here."

"That's good. And what does your dad do?" Russel asked and regretted it almost right away.

"My dad isn't around." Kyle took a deep breath and looked out the window. "It's my mom, my brother Timmy, who is five, and I."

"It's just my dad and I. My mom passed away in a lab accident when I was three," Russel said, his eyes fixed on the road. "Sorry if I'm over-sharing. I haven't actually talked to anyone besides my dad since the whole thing with Chelsea went down the drain."

"You're fine," Kyle said. "I think your breaking up with Chelsea was a blessing in disguise."

"I hope you're right."

"I am right," Kyle said confidently. "My house is right there at the end of the block. Thanks for the ride."

"Thanks for the invite," Russel said and unlocked the car doors. "I didn't expect to enjoy it as much as I did."

"No problem," Kyle said as he opened the door and stepped out of the car. "I'll see you on Monday."

Kyle slammed the door shut. Russel put his own address into the GPS and drove home with an unexpected thought in his head.

I want to be a pro-wrestler.

TWO

F elix rested in his favorite chair with the lights off. He let his body sink into the chair with his elbow resting comfortably on the soft handles. He had a glass of whiskey in his right hand. He savored every sip and was in no particular hurry to finish it.

It was half past eleven, and there was still no sign of Russel.

Just as thoughts of concern for his son's safety began to creep into his mind, a pair of familiar headlights flashed across the living room wall. Moments later, the car engine turned off, and Russel made his way up the stairs.

"Late night?"

"Jesus, Dad!" Russel cried out. His right hand went straight for the light switch. "Is it that much trouble to turn on the lights?"

"I needed to rest my eyes," Felix said. "You know I'm surrounded by bright lights, monitors, and people the entire day."

"I know, Dad. How was your meeting?" Russel asked and walked over to sit in an adjacent chair, leaving a round, glass coffee table between the two of them.

"It went very well," Felix said. "I'm going to have Alex work out the details, but this deal has the potential to be my most lucrative venture to date."

"You're going to sell that substance overseas?" Russel asked.

"I didn't commit to anything just yet," Felix said and took a sip of his whiskey. "We are going to do our due diligence before we enter into any kind of agreement."

"What's going to happen if you go through with this?"

"They are going to use this substance on the worst criminals in Japan."

"That still doesn't make it ethical," Russel insisted. "They can say they are using it on criminals, but are you going to be in Japan to actually make sure they don't use it for a selfish purpose?"

"I will have legal restrictions in place to make sure they can't just use it on anyone, son," Felix said and sat up in his chair. "I know how you feel about these things, but it's business."

"I know it's business Dad, but you're selling control in a bottle."

"It's for the greater good. It's going to revolutionize the prison system in Japan and quite possibly all over the world."

"I've had a long day," Russel said and pulled himself up out of the chair. "I'm going to bed."

"One day, the company will be yours Russel," Felix said, as his son began his ascent up the stairs.

"Goodnight, Dad," Russel called from upstairs.

Felix readjusted himself back into a comfortable position. His son always made valid points during their conversations, and while he didn't always agree, he appreciated his input. Russel was in a very small minority of people who spoke their minds when it came to Felix's business decisions. The vast majority of the people around him were yes men. They liked to tell him what they thought he wanted to hear.

His son had a good heart. A little too good. He knew Russel didn't get it from him.

He got it from his mother. She questioned a lot of his business dealings before her untimely passing. Even though she wasn't around to raise Russel, he stepped right into her shoes once he was old enough to understand how much power his father actually had.

———

"Kyle! Wake up honey, it's already ten o'clock! Do you really want to sleep away your entire weekend?" Janine Trevor asked, loud enough for her oldest son to hear upstairs in his bedroom.

"I'm up, I'm up," Kyle murmured just loud enough for his mom to stop shouting. He never understood why sleeping in a little on the weekend was seen as a crime in this house. Was it really a waste of the weekend if he got some extra rest?

He knew better than to bring up that issue with his mom. It would result in a very long *my house, my rules speech,* and that would be real waste of a weekend because he heard that speech at least twice a month as it was.

Kyle shoved his blanket off towards the wall and reluctantly rolled himself out of bed.Sitting up was absolutely out of the question the morning after a wrestling match. While he felt great the night of the show, everything from his back to his shoulders and quads was extremely sore the following morning. Some of it was just the wear and tear of being thrown around a ring that had some give, but not enough to say that landing on it was painless. Most of his morning aches could be attributed to the fact that he wrestled grown men on a weekly basis. As much as he had worked out and put on a solid ten pounds of muscle in the past year, he was still adjusting to the physical style of veteran performers like his mentor, Robert.

Kyle wouldn't have it any other way. He didn't believe in shortcuts. He wanted to work his way up from the bottom and pay his dues on the way to stardom. Besides, he was doing all of the right things in terms of taking care of his body.

"Before you storm up here," Kyle said and walked across the room towards the door that led into the hall. "I just want to let you know that I'm up. Just going to stretch for a few minutes."

"That's fine," Janine replied. "I did make you a batch of the protein pancakes, but if you take too long, Timmy might try to eat them."

Kyle shook his head and smiled. He bent down and started his stretch routine right away. His Mom wasn't joking. Timmy had quite an appetite for a five-year-old.

The stretching was only the beginning of Kyle's weekend routine. It would be followed by breakfast, and then he'd take Timmy to the park, where he would run a few laps to loosen up. After that, they'd head home, where Kyle would make lunch: sandwiches for Timmy, chicken breast, a baked potato, and salad for himself. He'd do some homework after lunch and then take a nap, as long as his mom didn't interfere. After the nap, he'd go down to the garage, which was by far his favorite part of the entire house. It's where Kyle put together the best gym a summer job could buy. He had a used dumbbell set, a squat rack, and a bench press. He needed everything to continue filling out his physique on days when he didn't have access to the school gym. There was also a set of three-pound dumbbells for Timmy. Since Janine worked overtime on most Saturdays during tax season, Timmy would spend most of the day under Kyle's supervision. The dumbbells were a perfect way for Timmy to keep busy while Kyle completed his work-out. Janine would arrive in time for dinner, and they would sit down to share a meal together.

That's usually when the questions would start.

"So, Kyle, no plans this Saturday night?" Janine asked.

"There were no shows in the area tonight," Kyle replied, hoping to avoid more questions.

"I didn't ask if there were shows tonight," Janine said. She looked over at Timmy's plate to make sure he ate his vegetables along with everything else. "There are other things to do besides training and wrestling on your days off."

"I have a goal in mind. You know that Mom," Kyle said, his eyes focused on baked ziti, one of Janine's Saturday night staples.

"Are the kids in school making fun of you for being a pro-wrestler?"

"No. That was a thing last year. Not so much this year." Kyle said.

Like most mothers, Janine was very concerned about her son being bullied in school. Kyle was aware of that. While he wasn't going around looking for trouble, he also wasn't going to be a punching bag for guys like Adam and Randy.

His serious demeanor made him seem somewhat unapproachable. He knew that it contributed to his lack of a real friend's circle, but he didn't lose sleep over it.

———

Kyle could feel the stares of a few guys from the football team as he pushed through the crowded hallways of Reign High School. He didn't particularly care. He stopped at his locker and peered down to make sure he put in the right combination.

"Did you take the air out of all of their footballs or something?" Vanessa asked.

"No," Kyle replied. "I did get in the way of their usual shenanigans."

"Care to elaborate?" Venessa asked. Her blonde hair was collected in a messy bun at the very top of her head and she was chewing her gum obnoxiously loud.

"They were picking on that new kid," Kyle said, digging through a mess of papers in his locker. "I sort of stepped in."

"Did you wrestle them to the ground?" Vanessa tried to keep a straight face, but by the time Kyle looked up, she was already laughing at her own joke. "Oh, relax tough guy! It's just a joke."

Vanessa had been Kyle's locker neighbor since freshman year. They could have been friends, perhaps something more, but Kyle never accepted any of her invitations to get together outside of school. The invitation became less and less frequent with every denial. Half way through their sophomore year, she gave up altogether. They remained locker neighbors and would chat most mornings. Vanessa admittedly did most of the chatting, but once in a while, Kyle would share something interesting with her. Today was one of those days.

"I talked with that kid Russel," Kyle said. "Apparently, he and Chelsea are done."

"That's such old news, Kyle," Vanessa said and shook her head. "I'm sorry. This is my fault. Sometimes, I forget that I'm the only person you actually talk to. I should have filled you in on the gossip."

"I talked with Russel."

"Would you have talked to him if he wasn't getting harassed by those tools?" Vanessa asked and motioned towards the football team a few doors down.

"Probably not," Kyle admitted.

"Here he comes. Maybe you'll make a friend? Miracles do happen, you know," Vanessa said and slammed her locker door shut with a surprising amount of force for a petite girl. "I'm going to class. I'll see you later."

Kyle watched Russel walk down the hall. He was looking down as always, with his hands buried deep into his pockets.

He's got to stop doing that, Kyle thought. *He is making himself a target and doesn't even realize it.*

Russel continued down the hall until he got to Kyle. "Hey Kyle, how's it going?" Russel asked. He slowed down briefly, but resumed his walk before Kyle said anything back.

"Russel! You got a minute?" Kyle asked, loud enough for the people around him to take notice.

Russel lifted his head and looked around before turning back. "Sure. What's up?"

"Listen. You need to stop doing that," Kyle said, looking directly at Russel.

"Doing what exactly?" Russel asked.

"Walking around with your head down like that," Kyle replied. "You're like the least intimidating six-foot tall person I've ever seen."

"I'm not trying to be intimidating."

"You seem like a good guy," Kyle said. "I can tell you don't want any trouble, but when you go from hanging out with the popular kids to walking around with your head down, it draws the attention of guys who want to seem tougher than they really are."

"Okay, I see what you're saying," Russel said. He took his hands out of his pocket and stood up straight. "I didn't realize I was even doing that."

"Looks like we are the same height," Kyle said. "You might even have an inch on me."

"Maybe there is something to this whole walking with my head held high thing," Russel said and cracked a smile.

Kyle nodded in agreement just as the morning bell rang.

———

The smell of the Reign High School Gym made the girls scrunch their noses as they strolled inside, but Kyle felt right at home there. The gym smelled great to him compared to some of the rundown venues and dirty rings he wrestled in on the weekends.

Kyle waved to the gym teacher, Mr. Ziggler, before making his way to the boy's locker room. Mr. Ziggler gave Kyle a warm smile that accentuated the wrinkles around his eyes and shifted his bushy eyebrows. He took a deep breath and rubbed what little, fine, silver hair he had left on the crown of his head. As in a lot of small High Schools, the gym teacher wore a few different hats. In Mr. Ziggler's case, aside from teaching Gym and Health, he also coached the boys' basketball team. For the better part of the past three years, he did everything in his power to convince Kyle to join the team. He didn't have much to show for his efforts. The boy was committed to wrestling. That didn't stop Mr. Ziggler from approaching Kyle before the start of every basketball season and seeing if he changed his mind. The answer was always no, but he did strike a deal with Kyle to come in during practices and run the drills and scrimmage with the team. In exchange, Kyle would have full access to the weights and machines after school, which were generally reserved for the school athletes.

Mr. Ziggler recognized that Kyle was in exceptional shape. He brought a certain intensity to every workout, and it was contagious. The other boys ran harder during suicides and played better defense when he was there.

"Kyle, we got the playoffs coming up in two weeks," Mr. Ziggler said.

Kyle walked along the baseline and met the teacher at half-court. "I hope this is the year for you guys," he said.

"You know I've been with the school for a long time," Mr. Ziggler said quietly. "I can pull some strings and get you on the playoff roster."

"You don't need me. You have a full roster, and those guys deserve the minutes."

"We could use you on defense," Mr. Ziggler said. "We have a few one-way players. They want to score, celebrate, and forget to run back on defense."

"I've heard," Kyle said and shook his head. "Look coach, I'd love to help you out, but I'm booked almost every weekend until May."

"I'm happy for you kid," Mr. Ziggler said and put his hand on Kyle's shoulder. "You're following your dreams, and I respect it."

"Thank you."

"Open gym today. I think the new kid needs one more on his team."

Kyle shifted his gaze towards the basketball hoops and spotted Russel right away. He was standing off to the side with Raymond, who was about a foot shorter than Russel and far from athletic. The opposing team was going to be in trouble, and not because Russel and Raymond were physically overmatched.

The team consisted of Randy, Adam, and their buddy Shawn. Kyle couldn't make out what was being said, but they were bouncing the ball aggressively, pointing at Russel and laughing.

Kyle bent each knee back and stretched his quads before walking towards Russel and Raymond with his sneakers squeaking against the gym floors. "You need one more?"

"I'm not sure I think these guys are waiting for someone," Russel said quietly as if hoping the other wouldn't hear him.

"Look at who we've got over here!" Adam announced. "The top three losers of the senior class, all on one team. What do you say we give them a shot at glory?"

"Gentlemen, I'm not really that good," Raymond said with a nervous smile. "I just wanted to shoot around."

"Raymond, when you step on this court, you've got to be ready to play!" Randy yelled.

"I'm actually on the sideline," Raymond said, and pushed his glasses up the bridge of his nose. "*Technically,* I'm not on the court."

"Technically, I might kick your ass!" Randy shouted and started stomping towards the much smaller Raymond.

"Easy there," Adam said. He put his hand on Randy's chest. Then he turned towards Kyle and Russel. "Are you losers in for this three on three? Or do you not want to participate in a *real* sport, Kyle?"

That was all Kyle needed to hear for his heart to start pumping. He felt his cheeks getting hot, and his breaths became deeper.

"I remember putting a certain football player into a *real* chokehold."

"Why, you little-"

Kyle picked up a ball and gave Adam a hard chest pass. "We are in. Your ball first."

Kyle looked over at Russel, who had stepped up to guard Randy. Adam pounded the ball against the wood floors, with his eyes fixed on Kyle.

"Raymond, you've got Shawn," Kyle said as he bent his knees and got into a defensive position.

Raymond nodded nervously. "I'll do my best."

Shawn gave Raymond a cocky smile. Shawn was even bigger than his teammates, with a broad back and legs as thick as tree trunks. He easily moved Raymond out of the way and posted up right under the basket. Adam recognized the obvious mismatch and dumped the ball to Shawn for an easy layup.

"That was all my fault guys," Raymond said.

"Don't worry about it," Russel said. He gave Raymond a pat on the shoulder and followed Kyle back on defense.

Adam tried to pass the ball to Shawn, expecting the same result, but Kyle saw it coming and intercepted the pass.

"Over here!" Russel called from the corner. His feet were squared towards the basket, and his hands were already in the position to catch and shoot.

Kyle passed the ball.

Swoosh!

"Okay, Russell!" Raymond said and ran over to give his teammate a high five.

"Good one," Kyle said, with significantly less enthusiasm. "Back on defense."

Adam gave Randy a dirty look before checking the ball to Kyle.

Russel tried to get open, but Randy was all over him this time. Kyle looked at Raymond, who was unsure of what to do. Kyle motioned for him to come closer, and he complied, with Shawn on his tail. Kyle passed Raymond the ball, pretended to run towards the left baseline, but instead cut toward the rim. "Raymond, bounce it!"

Raymond did as he was told and found Kyle right under the basket for what would have been a block for Adam, but Kyle jumped up high enough to finger-roll the ball right into the hoop.

Adam grabbed the ball and launched it against the wall. He checked it to Kyle breathing heavily and clenching his teeth.

Kyle bounced the ball between his legs a few times and then blew past Adam on his way toward the hoop. Randy quickly sagged off of Russel and came over to stop the lay-up. Kyle recognized the double team and tossed the ball towards Russel, who was open for a three pointer in the corner.

Russel took the shot and left his hand in the follow through position until the ball went through the net. He couldn't help but smile as he crossed the free-throw line with Kyle and Raymond.

"I'm pleasantly surprised," Kyle said.

"Good pass," Russel shrugged.

This time, the ball was passed to Russel. He didn't hesitate to give it to Raymond, who touch passed it right to Kyle.

Adam tried to swat the ball out of Kyle's hands. When that didn't work, he bumped Kyle with his chest and knocked him off balance. The distraction gave Adam a chance to snatch the ball away, but Kyle quickly recovered in time to play defense and not give Adam an open path to the basket.

"You can't stop me," Adam said. "I'll eat you up in the post!"

Kyle said nothing. Adam had at least thirty pounds on him, but he wasn't going to back down. Adam turned his back towards Kyle and attempted to back him down while dribbling the ball with one hand.

Russel was about to sprint over to help, but Kyle waved him off. "I've got this covered," he said.

Realizing that Kyle wasn't budging as easily as he had expected, Adam used his free arm to shove Kyle back far enough to give himself an open shot. The ball rattled around, with Russel and Randy tussling for position to get the rebound until the ball fell through the hoop.

"I told you," Adam said and shook his head at Kyle.

Russel dribbled the ball towards Kyle. "You're good?"

"Yeah," Kyle said. "Check it to Randy."

Russel did as instructed. Randy passed the ball off to Shawn who dribbled around aimlessly before finding Adam around the free-throw line.

Adam tried the same post-up move again, but this time, Kyle was able to reach in and almost stole the ball. Adam continued to pound the ball into the ground, trying to get a better position closer to the basket. Kyle dug in his heels and wouldn't budge.

Clearly frustrated, Adam picked up his dribble, stuck his elbows and turned his torso aggressively, striking Kyle in the face with his elbow. The impact sent Kyle stumbling backward with hands on his face.

Adam recognized the opportunity and ran in for an open layup.

Kyle didn't say a word. He bent over, holding his face. Blood was gushing out of his nose to the point where he couldn't contain it with his hands, both of which were completely red by this point.

Raymond remained still. Speechless.

"It's all part of the game," Adam said. He was smiling from ear to ear.

"Oh, is that so?" Russel asked and rushed towards Adam.

"What are you going to do about it, rich boy?" Adam asked, still smiling.

Russel walked right up to Adam, grabbed two fistfuls of his shirt and kneed him right in the stomach.

"Who do you think you are?" Randy asked, and shoved Russel towards Shawn who was by far the biggest one out of the group.

Shawn cocked back and punched Russel in the face sending him tumbling on the floor right next to Kyle.

"That's enough!" Vanessa shouted, and she pushed her way through the small crowd surrounding the scuffle. "Someone get Mr. Ziggler!"

Russel pushed himself up off the floor and blinked a few times while rubbing his face.

"Are you okay?" Vanessa asked. When Russel nodded, she kneeled down next to Kyle who was sitting against the wall. "You're still bleeding."

Randy and Shawn were smirking and giving each other high fives when Mr. Ziggler pushed past them and made his way towards Kyle and Russel. "What happened here?"

"The football team bench warmers were losing, so they decided to attack the other team," Vanessa said before anyone else could answer and glared at Adam.

The smirks on the football players' faces disappeared immediately.

"Vanessa, take the boys to the nurse please," Mr Ziggler said. "You three, I need to see you in my office."

"I didn't do anything!" Adam said and looked over at Randy for support.

"It was a complete accident!" Randy lied.

Vanessa gave Kyle a towel and escorted him and Russel out of the gym and up two flights of stairs, to the nurse's office.

Mrs. Rose was sitting behind her desk, flipping through the spring catalog. Her thick, oval shaped reading glasses complemented her curled, silver hair. The combination removed any doubt that she was by far the oldest member of the school faculty.

"Hello, Mrs. Rose," Vanessa said. "You've got two visitors."

Mrs. Rose dropped the catalog and jumped out of her seat at first sight of Kyle. "Oh, my dear boy! Who did this to you?"

Kyle tried to mumble something, but Vanessa cut him off and said, "It was one of the brutes from the football team."

"That's just awful," Mrs. Rose said and sat Kyle down on a chair next to her desk. She shifted her attention over to Russel. "And what happened to you?"

"If I could just get an ice pack for my face, I'll head back to class," Russel said.

"He got blindsided and punched in the face," Vanessa clarified.

Mrs. Rose opened a small freezer and took out an ice pack. "Here, take this and have a seat."

Russel grabbed the ice pack and placed it under his eye, where Shawn connected with quite a bit of force.

Kyle pulled his hands down. Mrs. Rose handed him a new paper towel. She quickly put on a pair of rubber gloves. She grabbed a paper towel of her own and wiped away the blood around the nose.

"Is the nose broken?" Russel asked as Kyle sat down in the chair next to him.

"The nose seems to be fine," Mrs. Rose replied, having wiped away most of the blood. "We'll just need to plug up the left nostril and keep his head tilted back for a few minutes."

"I'm fine," Kyle said with one eye open while Mrs. Rose plugged up his nostril.

"He is going to have to sit here for a few minutes," Mrs. Rose said as she collected the bloody paper towel around her desk. "Russel, if you're not dizzy, you and Vanessa can go back to class."

Russel nodded. "Kyle, I'll see you at lunch."

"I'm waving bye, Kyle," Vanessa said and waved even though he couldn't see her.

Kyle gave them a thumbs up with his head tilted back.

"You made friends with the new boy?" Mrs. Rose asked after Russel and Vanessa exited the office.

"Not intentionally," Kyle replied.

Mrs. Rose was friendly with a lot of the senior girls. They would come up to her office during lunch and fill her in on everything that was going on around the school. "A lot of friendships happen unintentionally. That boy needs a real friend. He never fit in with those hooligans that Chelsea hangs around with."

———

By the time lunch came around Kyle's nosebleed came to a halt. He walked into the lunch room and to a few stares and whispers, but he paid almost no attention to those things. As he passed Adam and Randy, the two of them stuffed tissue into their noses, laughed, and high fived each other, with a dozen of their football teammates laughing and clapping in support of their antics.

Kyle sat down and unzipped his lunch box, which contained a tuna salad, three hard boiled eggs, and an avocado. He didn't eat school lunches because he needed more nutrition in his meals to reach the peak physical condition and appearance that he desired.

Russel walked in just as Kyle began to peel one of the eggs.

"Is the nose feeling alright?" Russel asked. He stood by the table, tapping the floor with his left foot.

"It's okay. I've actually been kicked in the face before, so I've had worse," Kyle said. He looked up at Russel, who was still standing. "Do you want to sit? Or are you going to just stand there looking awkward?"

"I actually wanted to talk to you about something," Russel said.

"In that case, have a seat. I don't like when people stand over me unless it's part of a match," Kyle said and moved his lunch box closer to himself.

"Okay," Russel said. He sat down directly across from Kyle and took a deep breath.

"I have to ask you something first," Kyle said and began peeling one of the eggs. "Why did you step in during the scuffle earlier?

"It's hard to explain," Russel said. "I remembered you stepping in for me in the hall the other day when you didn't even know me."

"Why didn't you stand up for yourself that day then? You're clearly capable."

"It was different then. I was alone. It may sound corny to you, but I feel like we are a team. I want them to know if they mess with one of us, they are going to have to deal with us both."

"You're an interesting guy Russel," Kyle said with a nod of approval. "Well, what did you want to talk about?"

"I've been thinking about it over the weekend," Russel began. "And I've made up my mind. I want to be a wrestler."

Kyle stopped peeling his egg, looked up and raised his eyebrows. "What was that?"

"I want to be a wrestler. I saw what you were doing on Friday, and I want to do it too."

Kyle put his egg down and moved his lunch box aside. "Are you messing with me, Russel? Because today is not the day."

"No. I'm serious," Russel insisted. "I've been thinking about it all weekend. I could barely sleep last night because I was kind of nervous about telling you. I thought you'd laugh at me, but you seem more upset than anything."

"I'm not upset," Kyle said. "It's a joke to a lot of people here, but I take wrestling very seriously."

"I know. I would be lying if I said I'm a huge wrestling fan or that I always wanted to do it." Russel said. "But I think I could be good at it with the right guidance and training."

"I saw how you moved around on the court earlier," Kyle said. "You're more athletic than I thought."

"So, you're saying you'll train me?" Russel asked. His eyes lit up with excitement. Something that Kyle had never seen before.

"I didn't say all that," Kyle said and raised his hands in front of his chest. "I'm only two years in. I'm not qualified to train anyone."

"Oh, okay. It was worth a try. I'll see if I can find a wrestling school online or something."

"Don't waste your time. There are no good schools around here."

"So, what do you suggest I do?"

Kyle took a deep breath. "You remember Robert Crude?"

"Sure. The big guy you wrestled on Friday."

"He trained me. I can put in a good word for you," Kyle said and leaned forward. "But only if you're serious about it. Wrestling training is not a joke."

"I understand," Russel said. "I won't treat it as a joke."

"I'll give Rob a call tonight and see if he can get you in for a trial run this week."

"That would be awesome!" Russel said with a big smile sprawled across his face. "I really appreciate it, Kyle!"

"Don't thank me yet," Kyle said and shook his head. "At some point during that first day of training, you'll wish you hadn't asked me about this."

"We'll see," Russel said. He was excited about the prospect of wrestling training.

"Yes, we will," Kyle said. "I'll be there. I train with Rob three times per week."

"Even better!"

Kyle sighed and pulled his lunch box back towards himself.

This kid has no idea what he is getting into; he thought as he continued peeling the egg.

THREE

F elix stood up and faced the floor to ceiling window that provided the natural light in his office. He couldn't sit behind the mahogany desk all day, no matter how comfortable his chair was. Every few seconds he'd sneak a glance at one of his monitors. He was expecting a rather important email.

An alert popped up, and a split-second later, Alex walked into his office following a polite, yet completely unnecessary knock at the door.

"Come in Alex," Felix said. He took his seat behind the desk and opened the email.

Alex was Felix's right-hand man on all of the major deals. He was in his mid-twenties, very ambitious, and in some ways, reminded Felix of a younger version of himself. He had a full head of straight black hair that was brushed to the side. He was clean shaven, which emphasized a strong jawline and complimented his solid frame.

"I have the copies printed for you as we speak," Alex said. "But I know you wanted to take a look at everything as soon as possible."

"You know me well," Felix said. His eyes fixed on his monitor as he scrolled through all of the attachments.

"I do, Mr. Coleman," Alex said. Once again clutching his clipboard with one hand while straightening out his tie with the other. "That's why I've decided to come up here. I looked through all of the paper work as it was coming in. I don't think you should sign off on this deal."

Felix looked up from his monitor. "Alex, you disappoint me. Why would I pass up on a deal like this?"

"I did some research on Mr. Okada. There is a good reason for why his business partners turned their backs on him." Alex said.

"And what did you find?" Felix asked.

"He was forced out because he wanted to experiment on his own prisoners. Those androids aren't made from scratch. There is a theory that he used his prisoners, the ones with no family and no one looking for them, as test subjects."

Felix stroked his goatee. "Do you have any solid evidence?"

"Not yet-"

"Did my son put you up to this?"

"No. Mr. Coleman, look its-"

"Let me stop you right there Alex," Felix said and took a deep breath. "I called Mr. Okada a few minutes ago. It wasn't the easiest decision, but I informed him that I would not be moving forward with our joint venture. It might be a huge missed opportunity, but it would be far from being an ethical project. I want Coleman tech to change the world, and it's going to happen the right way. My late wife would never support a partnership between myself and Mr. Okada."

Alex smiled and nodded. "I think you're doing the right thing here."

"I wish there was this kind of money involved in more wholesome, humanitarian projects, but unfortunately, at the moment, that's simply not the case."

"I understand Mr. Coleman," Alex said. He did his best to sound sincere.

"I'll tell you what," Felix said in an upbeat tone. "With this project off the schedule, I have some free time. Why don't you forward me the plans you drew up for that underground self-sustaining farm facility? With all of the unrest in the world today, it might be a good time to develop a prototype."

"You're not messing with me, are you?"

"I'm not going to promise you anything," Felix said. "But I think that idea has legs. I'll let you take the lead on that project. You'll even have input on the location."

Alex found himself at the foot of the door with a sense of optimism followed by a wave of doubt. "I'm not sure I'm ready to lead that kind of project Mr. Coleman."

"Alex, listen to me," Felix said and leaned forward. "There are times to take a step back, and there are times to step up. This is the time to step up. You and I both know opportunities like this don't come around often."

"You're right," Alex replied. "I will put all the blueprints together tonight and go over everything with you tomorrow morning."

"Very well then," Felix replied. "Have a good night, Alex."

———

Kyle and Robert sat on the opposite corners of a dusty wrestling ring. They stretched everything from their calves to their shoulders, triceps and neck. Robert used to provide instructions on how to do every stretch, but it was no longer necessary with Kyle. He knew every stretch and every drill as well as Robert did.

The inside of the old, rusty garage served as Robert's training facility for up-and-coming wrestlers. It's where many lifelong wrestling fans and some of the toughest looking men and women came in to see if they had what it took to be professional wrestlers. The large majority of them threw their bodies against the steel ropes lined with a thin layer of rubber, followed by a few flat back bumps, and quickly realized that it wasn't for them.

Kyle was one of the people that bruised his back running against those same ropes and even strained his neck, taking his first flat back bump. Robert was convinced that the scrawny sixteen-year-old would lick his wounds and never step between the ropes again. He couldn't have been more wrong. Kyle came back the next day and attacked both the ropes and the mat with a rare intensity. While he wasn't a gifted athlete, he made up for it with hard work, consistency, and dedication. Kyle never took shortcuts and was always eager to learn. He quickly earned Robert's respect and became his number one trainee shortly after his arrival.

"I told him you'd give him a shot," Kyle said with his legs stretched in front of him and his fingers touching the toes of his wrestling boots.

"I give everyone a shot," Robert said. He was doing an identical stretch. "It just doesn't sound like he knows what he is getting into."

"He saw the entire card on Friday. He saw you throwing me around."

"I did throw you around quite a bit," Robert replied with a smirk. His clean, shaved head reflected the one bright light that illuminated the entire garage. He had a bushy beard, and boulder shaped shoulders to match the rest of his powerlifter physique. Unlike Kyle, he never had a problem putting on muscle mass. He did struggle following a strict diet, which was why Kyle had defined abs while Robert did not.

"I'll work with him on the partner drills," Kyle said and pulled himself up off the floor using the top rope.

"That's *if* we get to partner drills," Robert said.

"Here he is," Kyle said. He walked over, and gave Robert a hand to pull him up. "Let's get you up, old man. I know it's not as easy for you as it once was."

"Everyone's got a bump card kid," Robert said and gladly accepted the helping hand. "And mine is almost full."

"Hey Kyle," Russel said and took in his surroundings.

"Russel, this is Robert. Robert, Russel"

"Nice to meet you kid, formally this time," Robert said and extended his arm through the ropes.

Russel reached up for the handshake. "Same here. Great match Friday. I really enjoyed it."

"Nice, solid handshake. Always a good sign." Robert nodded in approval. "I'm glad you enjoyed the match, but I can almost guarantee you're not going to enjoy today's session."

"He is not joking," Kyle said and rolled his eyes.

"It's alright," Russel said. "I didn't come here to be babied. I came here to train."

"Then you came to the right place," Robert said. He sat on the middle rope and pulled up the top rope with one arm. "You're in for an experience of a lifetime."

Russel climbed up and stepped through the ropes. Kyle was already dressed in the ring, but this time, he was dressed in loose red shorts and a black T-shirt. No tights and no slicked back hair.

"We are going to start you off with the basics," Robert said and looked over at Kyle, who walked over to the middle of the ring. "Running the ropes."

Kyle took two big steps to his right, turned his back towards the rope and grabbed the top rope with his right hand. He bounced off the ropes, ran to the opposite side and did the same thing. Kyle continued to run the ropes until Robert motioned for him to stop.

"Okay, my turn," Russel said. He took a few deep breaths on his way to the middle of the ring.

"Now, remember to grab the top rope with your right hand every time," Robert said. "Okay, go ahead."

Russel ran at the ropes and tried to imitate Kyle. To his surprise, he wasn't bouncing off the ropes as easily. He could feel how clunky his movements were compared to Kyle, who glided from one side of the ring to the other. He continued to run until Robert stepped in and stopped him.

"That's enough for now," Robert said and put his arm around the young man's shoulder. "How do you feel?"

"A little winded," Russel admitted while gasping for air.

"The ropes will do that to you. Especially the first time." Robert said with a smile of satisfaction on his face. "Now, pay attention to what Kyle does. No one gets this perfect the first time, but you want to avoid messing up too much."

Once again, Kyle stepped to the middle of the ring. He dropped flat on his back with his knees bent and his hands flat on his side, clapping the mat as he made contact. He quickly turned to his right and used his forearm to push himself up off the floor almost immediately.

"Do you want me to show you again?" Kyle asked as if he hadn't just crashed onto the floor moments earlier.

"I think I get the gist of it," Russel said and approached the middle of the ring with hesitation.

"Now listen kid," Robert said. "You want to tuck your chin on the way down. The last thing you want is whiplash or a concussion on your first day of training."

Russel tried to imitate Kyle's quick fall and implement Robert's tips into his first attempt. All that amounted to was an awkward landing on his side and lower back, with hands hitting the floor long after his body did. He felt pain shooting up his back.

He rolled over gingerly and laid on his stomach before using both of his hands to push himself up. He failed miserably and collapsed back onto the floor. "I'm okay," he muttered.

Kyle walked over and stood over him. Then looked back at Robert. "We've seen worse," he said and shrugged his shoulders.

"Alright, kid," Robert said with renewed enthusiasm. "Let's take it from the top. I need nine more flat back bumps!"

Russel grabbed onto the rope and used it to pull himself up. "Okay, you got it," he said and hobbled back towards the middle of the ring.

————

Felix stepped into the quiet hum of the elevator and pressed the button for the basement. It was part of his daily routine to go down to the gym after a long day of phone calls, meetings, and contract signings. Every day at around six, all of that would stop, and he would change into his sweatpants and sleeveless shirt and head for the gym.

The elevator came to a halt, and Felix stepped out to find the gym completely empty. He wasn't surprised. Every single employee of Coleman Tech had full access to the gym, yet Felix worked out alone almost every night. He didn't mind the solitude. He welcomed it.

Felix's workouts didn't include any music. He didn't even own a pair of headphones. He preferred to work out in complete silence. He didn't need any distractions. He needed to remain focused on the task at hand.

His workouts always began with extensive stretching. He believed it was the key to avoiding injury, which was what he managed to do throughout the duration of his adult life. At forty-four years old, Felix had never been in better shape. He knew part of it was his genetics, and that was why his son, who wasn't a fitness enthusiast, was somehow still in above average shape. Most of it was discipline. Felix went down to the gym Monday through Friday. It didn't matter if the meetings ran late; he'd go down to the gym as soon as everything wrapped up. He also never ate junk food and followed a strict diet that allowed him one cheat meal per week.

Once he stretched the muscles and warmed up his joints, Felix moved on to his favorite part of the workout; the weights. Years of training taught him to start with lighter weights. He grabbed twenty-pound dumbbells and did a few reps of incline chest press. Once he felt his muscles activate, he'd move on to the seventy-pound dumbbells for the next set and would increase the weight by five pounds with every set after that.

There were no shortcuts and no extended breaks. Felix would do six to ten different workouts, four sets of everything, with no exceptions. There were only one minute breaks in between sets and even shorter breaks between exercises because he always knew exactly what he was doing next.

During the breaks, Felix's mind would occasionally drift to his son. He was concerned about Russel. The boy had a good heart. He was afraid it was too pure for the unforgiving world that he was growing up in. He also knew there wasn't much he could do to change his son's perspective on life, and he knew exactly why. Even though Felix raised Russel, he inherited a lot of traits from his mother.

Felix met Marissa in college. It wasn't love at first sight, but the two of them worked together on numerous projects, and before they knew it, their professional relationship blossomed into a romantic one. They got engaged the summer after college and were married a few months after that. They agreed not to have kids right away and spent the first five years of their marriage building up Coleman Tech from the ground up.

Marissa was in charge of the science department, while Felix spearheaded the business side of the company. Marissa had created the blueprint for many of the projects that Coleman Tech was working on fifteen years after her untimely passing, including the substance that Felix had almost contracted out to Mr. Okada. She was a genius, but she was also the person who kept Felix in check. She always warned him not to go into business with people who might use their creations to hurt others. He always listened to her, even if it sometimes meant passing up on a big money deal.

It's been fifteen years, Felix thought to himself. He sat up on the bench press with his elbows on his knees. Steady drops of sweat worked their way from his forehead into his goatee and eventually onto the floor. Fifteen years after his wife lost her life in that tragic accident, and it still haunted him.

He was in a meeting when he received the call about an explosion. He didn't think much of it; there were small lab fires every few months. No one was ever seriously hurt. This fire was very different.

An unstable compound wasn't contained properly. By the time Marissa realized what was happening, it was too late. The explosion consumed the entire lab facility and the three buildings around it. When Felix made it to the lab building, there was no building left to speak of.

Marissa had to be identified using her teeth. It was the second worst experience of Felix's life.

The first was having to tell his three-year-old son that Mommy was never coming home.

Felix got under the barbell on the squat rack and performed a few heavy squats. The three hundred fifteen pounds on his shoulders, combined with the burning of his quads, helped tune out the pain of having to relive that day all over again.

Felix slammed the barbell back into place and took a few steps back. He was breathing heavily with his hands on his hips. He wondered if he would have entertained the idea of signing the deal with Mr. Okada if Marissa was still around.

He shook his head and stepped in for another set. He couldn't think like that. As he lowered himself towards the floor for another squat, he reminded himself that he was doing this for their son. Everything that he did was to create the best possible life for Russel. He had to believe that Marissa would be okay with that.

———

"Okay, bring it in!" Robert said. He waved the boys over.

Kyle and Russel rolled out of the ring and towards Robert who was sitting on a metal folding chair outside of the ring with his arms crossed. "That wasn't bad for the first day, Russel."

Russel struggled to catch his breath. "Thank you," he whispered and bent down with his hands on his knees.

Kyle's shirt was drenched in sweat after grappling with Russel, but he was breathing just fine. He took pride in his conditioning, and it would take a lot more than an hour in the ring to tire him out.

"Kyle," Robert said and raised his eyebrows. "Any thoughts on the new kid?"

"You're naturally athletic," Kyle said. "I saw it during our brief basketball game. That's the main reason for why I agreed to bring you here."

"That's as much of a compliment as you'll get out of this guy," Robert said.

"If you're serious about doing this," Kyle said and looked over at Russel, who managed to stand up straight. "You'll need to work on your conditioning. The first thing an opponent will try to do to a new guy is try to blow him up."

"He ain't lying, kid," Robert nodded. "The guys at the YMCA tried to do it to him a few times with little success."

"Okay, I'll work on it," Russel said.

"Overall, you did a good Russel," Kyle said and glanced over at Robert. "I'm going to finish up, Rob."

"Go right ahead," Robert said.

Kyle made his way around the rings and through the black curtain to the rear of the garage space.

"He is not done?" Russel asked.

"Kyle? No. He is always the last one to leave. I used to wait for him, but I've got a wife and two kids waiting for me at home. I gave him his own set of keys."

"I feel like we did a pretty good workout."

"You did," Robert said. "All of my students go through the routine that you and Kyle went through today. Then Kyle stays for another forty-five minutes."

"What does he do?"

"He usually does five hundred hack squats, five hundred push-ups and a variation of his abs workout," Robert said with a smile on his face.

"He does all of that?" Russel asked, wiping the sweat from his forehead. "After all of the running and bumping that we just did?"

"Bumping? Look at you picking up wrestling lingo!" Robert said. He stood up and folded his chair. "To answer your question, yes. He does all that, and he has a reason for it. You know he said you were naturally athletic?"

"Yeah."

"Well, he knows because he is not."

"What do you mean? He moves better than me. He's explosive, too! Threw me right across that ring like a rag doll." Russel said. His eyes shifted from one side of the ring to the other.

"He wasn't always like that," Robert said. "When he first got here, he could barely do a barrel roll. I was convinced he wasn't going to make it past the first week. But he continued to work, and he outworked everyone here. Everything you saw in that ring is a product of hours upon hours of Kyle pushing himself to the limit."

"That's impressive," Russel said.

"I know. I have a lot of respect for that kid. That's why I agreed to give you this little try out." Robert said. "Kyle wouldn't bring someone here unless he saw something in you."

Russel didn't know what to say about that, so he remained silent.

"Anyway, it's getting late. Let's get going." Robert said and headed for the gates. "He likes to be left alone for this part of the workout."

FOUR

Much to Robert's and Kyle's surprise, Russel stuck with the training. After four weeks, he looked better than most of Robert's recruits after four months. At the start of the fifth week, Robert approached Kyle with a proposition.

It was the end of another training session. Russel went to the bathroom to change, and Kyle was somewhere in the middle of his five hundred hack squats.

Robert walked in with his favorite chair, unfolded it a few feet away from Kyle and sat down with his arms crossed. "You know next month's show is set to have our biggest crowd of the year."

"That's great," Kyle said with a grunt.

"The big draw is the tag team tournament."

"What's that got to do with me?" Kyle asked. He continued squatting at a steady pace.

"What do you say we put you in a tag team?" Robert countered.

"No. I know what you're thinking, and I'm not going for it."

"I'm just throwing some ideas out there. That's all."

Kyle stopped squatting and walked over towards Robert. "You want to put me with the newbie, and that's a terrible idea."

"Hear me out," Robert said. He stood up and put his arm around

Kyle's sweaty shoulder. "The kid is a natural. We both see it. It'll be for an opening match, and I'll put you with one of the experienced tag teams to make it even easier."

"You're asking me to step into a role that I'm not meant to fill, "Kyle said. "I'm not a team player, and I'm definitely not a leader."

"I believe you can be," Robert insisted.

"Robert, there are nine other guys-"

"You don't get along with any of them!" Robert exclaimed. "Teams need chemistry, and the only one you seem to get along with here is Russel."

Robert had a valid point. Kyle didn't mingle with any of the other guys, just like he didn't really have any close friends in school. On the other hand, he and Russel spent quite a bit of time together carpooling to and from wrestling school. Kyle was opposed to it at first, but gas wasn't cheap, and his funds as a high school senior were limited. Russel joined Kyle after class, and they would go through his post-class workout together on most days. They sat together at lunch as well. Russel had a lot of questions about wrestling history and psychology, and if there was one thing Kyle didn't mind talking about, it was wrestling.

"Okay, I'll tell you what," Kyle said as he resumed squatting. "I will think about it tonight. I still don't think it's a good idea, but I do think it would be a good first match for him."

"My point exactly!" Robert said, unable to contain his excitement.

"I didn't say yes." Kyle insisted.

"I know you well enough," Robert said. "You'll warm up to the idea because you know some of wrestling's biggest stars started out in tag teams. So why not you?"

Kyle wiped the sweat from his brow and resumed squatting.

He didn't have to look at Robert to know that he walked out past the curtain with a smile on his face.

———

The next day at lunch, Russel got his food and took his usual seat across from Kyle, who was already halfway through his lunch.

"Well, someone was hungry," Russell said.

"I went for a run this morning before class," Kyle said.

"Of course, you did," Russel said. He started on his own lunch.

"Did Robert say anything to you?" Kyle asked.

"No. Why?"

"There is a spot open for a tag team on next week's card," Kyle said with little enthusiasm. "He wants to book me for it."

"That's great! I was talking to one of the guys in our class and they said the tournament is a bigger deal than the main event." Russel said. "Who are you partnering up with?"

Kyle fixed his gaze on Russel but didn't say a word.

"No way!" Russel said and jumped out of his seat. "You're joking!"

"Will you keep it down?" Kyle said. Russel's sudden burst of excitement turned a few heads.

"I'm sorry," Russel said and sat back down. "I wasn't expecting that at all."

"I'm going to be honest with you," Kyle said. "You're still green."

"Green as in…"

"Green, as in you're still inexperienced," Kyle explained. "Yes, you're way better than most people after only a month of training. You're definitely way ahead of where I was at this point in my training."

"I think this is going to be good for both of us," Russel said. He was smiling from ear to ear. "I won't let you down."

"I know, but we have to lay out the match in a way-"

"And we will," Russel cut him off. "Right now, I need to go call my Dad. He has no idea I've been doing this, and I feel like he should probably be there for my first match."

"You didn't tell him? Where does he think you go four times a week for three hours?"

"I told him I just go to the gym," Russel said and shrugged his shoulders. "I'm not sure he'll be supportive of this idea. But I think telling him is the right thing to do."

"Most parents aren't too crazy about their kids becoming professional wrestlers," Kyle said. "My mom certainly wasn't."

"Was she at your first match?"

"She was," Kyle said and cracked a rare smile. "Okay, go call your dad."

————

Russel never got past his dad's secretary, who insisted that he was in a very important meeting. She offered to put him through, but only if it was an emergency. Russel politely declined and opted to tell his dad about it when they were home later that night.

He didn't want to rattle his dad in the middle of a meeting. He was fairly certain that this revelation wasn't going to go over well, at least not at first.

Felix had a specific plan in place for his son. Becoming a professional wrestler was not part of it, even if it was only a hobby at this point.

Russel drove home and rehearsed what he was going to tell his Dad. In the back of his mind, he knew the conversation wasn't going to go as he had planned. He could only hope that his dad would be at least somewhat understanding.

Russel sat down in his usual spot, the comfortable chair opposite from where Felix always sat, usually with his glass of whiskey.

He heard the car pull into the parking lot, and his dad walked up the stairs moments later.

"Russel, it's good to see you at home before dark, son." Felix said he had taken off his suit jacket and loosened his tie. "Is everything alright?"

"Yeah, everything is fine, Dad. I just wanted to talk to you about something."

"We can do that," Felix said. He hung his coat on the back of the chair closest to him and joined his son at the coffee table.

"Okay, Dad, it's nothing crazy," Russel began. "But I've started pro wrestling training, and I'm going to have my first match this Friday."

"Pro wrestling?" Felix asked and leaned forward. "How did you start pro wrestling? I don't remember you ever doing amateur wrestling."

"That's not how it works," Russel said with a nervous laugh.

"You didn't think to ask me first before doing this?"

"It just sort of happened, Dad. I didn't expect to be any good at it, but I caught on very quickly."

"I've noticed that you've started eating better and that some of my protein powder was missing," Felix said, looking down at the coffee table. "I would have never guessed it's because you decided to train for wrestling, of all things."

"It was kind of unexpected for me too," Russel admitted. "I made a friend in school who has been doing it for two years. I asked him if he knew anyone that could train me and it just kind of took off from there."

"You're sure he didn't try to convince you? Who is this friend?"

"He didn't. He was actually skeptical about the whole thing," Russel said. "His name is Kyle Trevor. He is a really good guy. I think you would get along with him."

"You made a new friend," Felix said. He stroked his goatee with one hand. "That's great. I was beginning to worry."

"No need to worry, dad. Everything is fine."

"Everything is not fine, son." Felix said. "You made a pretty big decision without consulting me first."

"I didn't expect for-"

"I don't care what you expected. In this house, all the decisions go through me."

"Okay. I'm sorry," Russel said and sank into his chair.

"I don't know the first thing about pro wrestling," Felix continued. "But it doesn't sound safe."

"I'll be really careful." Russel paused in case his dad decided to go on with the lecture. When he didn't, Russel said, "My first match is Friday night. I'd really like it if you were there."

"This is coming on a very short notice, Russel. And I'm not very happy with you right now." Felix said and stood up. "I'll try, but I can't make any promises."

"Fair enough," Russel said. He sighed in relief and made his way upstairs to his room.

Felix remained in the living room. He poured himself a glass of whiskey and walked over to the living room window to admire the sunset. He took a few sips and then reached down into his right pocket for his phone. It was almost eight o'clock, but he was hoping Alex was still available.

He clicked on his name and brought the phone up to his ear.

"Hello?" Alex answered after one ring.

"Alex, I need you to do me a quick favor."

"Sure. What is it?" Alex asked.

"I need you to go through our databases and get me everything you can on a local kid named Kyle Trevor," Felix said.

"Okay. Are we bringing him in for an interview?"

"No. Just get me everything you have and forward it to my email."

"No problem Mr. Coleman. I'll have it done right away."

"Thank you, Alex," Felix said and hung up.

———

Kyle took match preparations very seriously, but he was going to be extra diligent when it came to this tag team match. Their opponents were the Cross Brothers. An up-and-coming tag team with about five years in the business. Robert gladly provided the Cross Brother's phone number and Kyle called them up to talk about the match. He explained that this would be Russel's first match and that they would need to take things slow.

The brothers were good sports about it. They agreed to discuss the details of the match before the show started on Friday. They would be going over; they were booked to win the match and move on to the next round of the tag team tournament. Kyle had no problem with that. His only concern was getting through the match safely and putting on a show for the crowd.

Everything was going smoothly until Friday afternoon when Russel came to Kyle with an idea for their match.

Kyle was sitting in the locker room with the Cross Brothers. They were going back and forth with their ideas for the match, while the brothers put handfuls of conditioner into their long, thick, curly hair to give themselves the classic wet hair look.

Russel brushed past wrestlers of various shapes and sizes before he made it to Kyle and the Cross Brothers. They were sitting on the opposite locker room benches. Kyle was doing the talking with his elbows resting on his knees.

"Hey guys, am I late?" Russel asked.

"No, you're fine," Kyle said. He motioned for Russel to join him on the bench. "Larry, Kurt, meet my partner. This is Russel."

They nodded politely and took turns giving Russel a fist bump. Their hands were still wet with what seemed like a never-ending supply of conditioner.

"Nice to meet you guys," Russel said and took a seat next to Kyle. "I don't mean to interrupt, but I have an idea."

All eyes shifted to Russel. It was unusual for rookies to have significant input on their debut matches.

"What's the idea?" Kyle finally asked.

"I want to do a shooting star press tonight," Russel announced.

Kurt and Larry paused their conditioning routine and gave each other a bewildered look.

Kyle rubbed his eyes and said, "Russel, a shooting star press is a dangerous move."

"I know. I've been practicing it on the dummy before joining your post workout routine."

"And you got full rotation on the backflip and landed flat on the dummy every time?"

"Not the first few times, but this whole week, I've been hitting it with ease," Russel said proudly.

"If he can do it," Kurt said and looked at his brother for approval. "We'll take it."

"I don't think it's a good idea," Kyle insisted.

"The kid wants to make an impression," Larry said. "I think we'd be doing the crowd a disservice by not letting him do it."

"I'm not okay with this," Kyle said with a sigh. "I don't think you should do it."

"It'll get a huge pop from the crowd," Russel said. "It'll set our match apart from all of the other matches on the card."

"I like the way the newbie thinks," Kurt said.

The shooting star press would be a moment to remember, but not for the intended reason.

———

Felix was a big believer in preparation and organization. He knew no other way of doing business. He valued his own time, as well as the time of his business partners and employees. His preparedness and time management allowed him to maximize his free time.

On this particular Friday, that resulted in finishing up early and having time to race down to the YMCA for his son's debut match.

He had no choice but to skip his workout. A rare occasion, but some things were more important than his physique. Being there for his son was one of them.

Felix rushed past a dozen of his employees on the way and told each one of them to have a good weekend before he hopped in his car and raced to the other side of town. When he arrived, there were no readily available parking spaces. He scanned the street for a spot and found one that was just big enough to fit his car if he maneuvered it correctly. Luckily Felix had years of experience driving and parking in areas such as Brooklyn, New York. There was no such thing as a big parking spot there, and every inch counted.

He parked his car on the first attempt and headed for the entrance. There was no line or crowd outside. There was only an older gentleman with bushy white eyebrows and a matching mustache, wearing an oversized jacket that read SECURITY in white letters on the front.

"Sorry, pal. The show is sold out." He called out when Felix got within shouting distance.

"Is it really?" Felix asked and reached into his pocket for a thick wad of cash. He took out a crisp one-hundred-dollar bill and handed it to the man guarding the door.

"I guess we have some standing room available," the security guard said. His eyes lit up as he grabbed the bill and let Felix walk right past him. "Enjoy the show!"

Felix arrived just in time to see his son walk out to the ring to an extremely loud song, which he was completely unfamiliar with. Russel was dressed in a tight, black sleeveless shirt, black tights, and white wrestling boots. His hair was slicked back to match his partner who was walking right next to him. Russel looked nervous, which in turn, made Felix nervous. Kyle was high fiving the people in the front row and seemed to be right at home in this environment.

The security guard wasn't joking when he said the event was sold out. There wasn't a single open seat. Felix found a spot that offered acceptable visibility behind the last row of seats. He leaned against the wall and watched his son climb into the ring.

Russel walked around the ring and pulled on the ropes. They were a lot tighter than the ones at Robert's wrestling school.

Kyle motioned for Russel to join him in their corner. "I'm going to start the match. Whenever I get close to the corner, you reach out over the top rope for the tag. Got it?"

Russel nodded anxiously.

"I'm going to do about four minutes. Then I'm going to tag you in, and you're going to do exactly what we talked about. If you get lost, just grab a headlock, and they'll tell you what to do next."

"Okay. Let's do this." Russel said. He climbed to the outside of the ring and stood in the corner.

Kyle and Larry started the match with a traditional lock up. Kyle had about an inch on Larry, but the latter made up for it in muscle. He quickly threw Kyle into the corner and gave him a few punches to the head before Kyle ducked out and delivered a few punches of his own.

Larry shoved Kyle, forcing him to backpedal towards the middle of the ring. The two of them locked up again, but only this time, Kyle was the one on the offensive. He kicked Larry in the gut, bounced off the ropes and used the momentum to shoulder tackle Larry. He was unsuccessful, and Larry remained standing but wobbling. Kyle ran back toward the rope with even more force and attempted the shoulder tackle again. This time, he sent Larry to the ground.

Russel anxiously followed every move. He knew exactly what he had to do once Kyle gave him the hot tag. His heart would race every time Kyle got close to their corner, even though he knew exactly when it would be his turn.

Kyle stayed on the offensive until Larry slipped away from and tagged in his brother. Kurt was by far the biggest competitor in the match and threw Kyle from corner to corner with relative ease. Kyle made a few attempts to reach Russel's outstretched arm, but Kurt prevented him from making the tag every time. Finally, Kyle managed to trap Kurt in a head-lock, giving him the opening that he needed to reach Russel for the hot tag.

Kurt struggled to get out, and eventually, he did, but by that point, Russel received the much anticipated hot tag. The crowd applauded and whistled when he stepped between the ropes. He and Kyle performed a double team maneuver, a double shoulder tackle that landed Kurt flat on his back.

"You got this, Russel," Kyle whispered. He rolled out of the ring and made his way to their corner of the ring.

Russel took a deep breath and performed the moves in the order that was discussed in the locker room. A few punches to the head, followed by a clothesline, and once Kurt made it back to his feet, Russel gave him the neck breaker, leaving Kurt laying on his back in the perfect position for the shooting star press.

Russel walked to the turnbuckle and scaled the ropes until he climbed to the very top. He positioned himself for the jump and looked over at Kyle. He was clapping along with the crowd, but his facial expression was uneasy.

Russel took another deep breath. He stood up straight and jumped in the air. All he remembered thinking was that he was coming up short on the rotation on the way down.

The crowd let out a collective, "Oooohhhhhh!"

It wasn't the positive reaction everyone involved was hoping for.

Russel failed to complete the rotation and landed awkwardly on his neck.

The referee remained almost invisible throughout the match, ran over to Russel, dropped to his knees and whispered something to Russel. When there was no response, he looked at Kyle in distress and shook his head slowly. He proceeded to throw up the X symbol with his arms, which sent the paramedics rushing through the crowd.

Kyle was frozen in his corner. He knew something terrible had

STOLEN RING TIME   51

happened, but even with all of the commotion around him, he was unable to move.

Felix rushed to the ring as soon as his son landed with a thud. He might not have known wrestling, but he knew of a bad accident when he saw one. "Out of my way!" He yelled as he shoved people with both arms.

He was met by a chubby security guard at the rail. "Sir, we are going to have to ask-"

"Step aside! That's my son in there!" Felix said.

"Let him through," the referee called from the ring.

By the time Felix hopped the rail and ran up the stairs into the ring, the paramedics had Russel on a stretcher.

"How is he?!" Felix asked.

"He is breathing," one of the paramedics replied. "But we need to get him to a hospital quickly!"

The two paramedics motioned for everyone to get out of the way as they slid Russel's stretcher across the ring until they got to the ropes. Then, the two of them rolled out of the ring and gently picked up the stretcher, transferring it to the ground.

Felix continued to shove the curious fans aside until he made it out of the building, along with the paramedics and Russel.

Kyle remained in his corner.

"Hey, kid!" Robert said. He slid into the ring and put his right hand on Kyle's shoulder. "It wasn't your fault."

Kyle didn't say a word. All he could think about was how excited Russel was to perform the risky stunt and how he didn't do enough to stop him.

————

There was a ride to the hospital, and there were people rushing past him going both ways in the hallway, but Kyle remembered none of that. He was completely numb to everything happening around him.

"Kyle, honey it's Mom." Janine said. She took her son's right hand with both of hers. "I heard about what happened."

"It was my fault," Kyle said with a blank stare. "I should have talked him out of it."

"It's not your fault. It was an accident," Janine said, and she squeezed her son's hand a bit tighter.

Kyle shook his head and continued to stare at nothing in particular.

He sat there, hoping to hear some good news. Any news at all. The doctors gave no update.

Robert busted through a set of double doors and rushed towards Kyle and Janine. "Hello, Ms. Trevor, Kyle. We should probably head for the exit."

"Why is that?" Janine asked.

"Because," Robert said and looked back. "Mr. Coleman is on the way and he is on quite a rampage. He got into a fight with security downstairs, but I don't think they'll be able to hold him for long."

"Surely he doesn't blame Kyle for-"

"I'm not sure," Robert admitted and shot another glance towards the door. "But I don't think this is the time or the place for Mr. Coleman and Kyle to discuss what went wrong earlier."

"Your friend is probably right," Janine said. She stood up and pulled her son out of the chair. "Let's get you home."

"I'll stay here in case there are any updates," Robert said. "Head down the hall and make the second left. That staircase will take you right to the parking lot."

"Thank you, Robert," Janine said. She put her hand on her son's back and led him out of the building.

———

The sun was beginning to creep in through the window when Felix took the last remaining sip of the whiskey he had stashed in his office. It was there for celebratory purposes.

The signing of a big contract. Or the completion of a long project.

On this particular morning it was used to numb the pain and uncertainty that was brought on by the incident involving Russel the night before.

His son remained in the hospital overnight. He had a broken neck, and his condition was uncertain, to say the least. The doctors said there was some brain damage, and the best course of action would be to wait for the swelling to go down.

Felix found himself in his office, reaching out to his connections in the medical field. He was hoping someone would give him some hope. He slammed the phone more times than he cared to count when no one told him anything remotely close to what he wanted to hear. At that point, Felix grabbed hold of his favorite whiskey bottle, and the rest of the night turned into a blur.

He felt tremendous guilt and anger. Perhaps if he had been more available to spend time with his son, then he wouldn't have turned to doing those dangerous stunts in that ring. So many what -if scenarios crossed his mind that he began to feel a headache coming on. He told himself it was the effect of the alcohol, or maybe the stress and uncertainty of what had taken place. It was likely a mix of everything and Felix saw no light at the end of this dark tunnel.

Just as Felix was about to attempt to pull himself up and out of his chair, the office phone rang. Felix glanced over at it but didn't pick up. *Who would be calling here on a Saturday morning?* He thought to himself as he reached for the phone.

"Hello?" he finally answered after the fourth ring.

"Mr. Coleman," said a vaguely familiar voice. "I've been trying to reach you for almost an hour."

"Mr. Okada," Felix muttered and sat up. "My cell phone must have died. What can I do for you?"

"I heard about what happened with your son," Mr. Okada said with a hint of remorse. "I am truly sorry."

"Thank you," Felix said. He rubbed his left temple with his hand, hoping it would alleviate the pounding in his head. It did nothing. "How did you hear about it? If you don't mind me asking."

"Word travels fast in this day and age," Mr. Okada replied. "I'm calling you because I might be able to help."

Felix's heart started to beat at an alarming rate. He was fully alert before Mr. Okada finished the sentence. "You have my undivided attention."

"I must warn you," Mr. Okada began. "I cannot guarantee your son's full recovery. What I can offer you is a chance to bring your son back from the brink of death."

"That's more than what anyone else has been willing to offer me."

"So I've heard."

"Well, what is it?" Felix asked impatiently.

"My company has an experimental regeneration program. We use it to revive certain parts of the human body that have been damaged severely. As you've probably guessed by now, we use it on our android subjects."

Felix took a deep breath and rubbed the bridge of his nose with his free hand. "You're suggesting that we turn my son into an android?"

"No." Mr. Okada replied. "I'm only suggesting that we use my technology to help your son. The thing is Mr. Coleman, we've never used it to restore a broken neck or damaged brain function. It would take a lot of diligent work and most importantly time."

"What have you used this technology on?" Felix asked. "And how much time are we talking about here?"

"Its primary use has been to restore limbs and a few internal organs." Mr Okada said. "Those things only take a few months to become functional. Sometimes a year."

"How long would Russel's injury take?"

"We'd have to run a simulation," Mr. Okada said. "My estimation would be about twenty years."

"Twenty years…" Felix said. "You're telling me I won't see my son for twenty years, and you can't even guarantee a full recovery?"

"I'm saying this is an option that I can offer you," Mr. Okada said. "If someone out there has a better offer for your son, then I expect you to take it."

"No one has made any offers Mr. Okada. I have an eighteen-year-old with swelling of the brain and a broken neck!" Felix yelled into the phone.

"I understand." Mr. Okada said, unphased by Felix's outburst.

"Hold on," Felix said. He took a moment to collect himself. "Let's just say that I agree. What is this going to cost me?"

"I need you to enter into the previously discussed partnership with me." Mr. Okada said. "We'll be equal partners. Just like we discussed in our first meeting."

"That's all?" Felix asked.

"Just one more thing. I'll need to move the project to your head-quarters in Reign."

"And why is that?"

"A few reasons." Mr. Okada said. "First and foremost, you'll want to be close to your son to monitor his progress."

That was all Felix needed to hear.

Unlike everyone else Felix reached out to, Mr. Okada was able to give him hope for a future with his son. He would do whatever it took to make sure that Russel resumed his life, whether it happened in a year or in two decades.

FIVE

K yle never received the positive news he was hoping for in regards to Russel. All he heard was the talk around town that the day after the injury, his dad stormed the hospital for a second time and had him transferred to a private facility that was set up at Coleman Tech.

It had been nearly two days since Russel's ill-fated shooting star press. Kyle was barely able to sleep, and he had no appetite. He never dealt with anything like this before. He decided he couldn't just stay home and think about what happened. He packed his gym bag and jogged three miles to Robert's school for a workout.

By the time he opened the garage door, he was sweating profusely.

This is good, he told himself. *Maybe I can work up an appetite.*

He walked past the ring but was unable to get inside. Images of Russel's landing were still haunting him. He knew he'd have to get past it eventually, but he wasn't ready just yet. The weights seemed a lot more inviting. After a brief stretch, Kyle laid down on the bench and pressed the equivalent of his body weight for ten reps. He sat up and took in the burning in his chest and shoulders.

Kyle grabbed the jump rope without taking a break and began to jump without counting. He felt a tingling sensation in his arms and calves, but he didn't let that stop him. He closed his eyes and kept going. Images of Russel's landing seeped into his mind. All he could do was increase the speed of the rope, forcing his body to keep up. He kept going until all he could feel was the burning in his muscles. The rope got caught on his heel, forcing him to stop. He threw the rope aside and laid back down on the bench press. He pumped out another set of ten before jumping rope once again.

After three more rounds, Kyle had no choice but to take a break.

He sat on the bench with his heart pounding. He was dripping with sweat which was rolling off of his hair and into his eyes.

He brushed his hair back with one hand and looked up when a long shadow stretched across the pavement outside the garage doors. Kyle looked on as the shadow shrunk. He wasn't expecting any visitors, nor did he want any. Once the shadow disappeared, Vanessa stepped through the garage doors.

Kyle stood up and walked to her. "Vanessa? What are you doing here?"

"Hey Kyle," she said. She had her hair down, and she brushed it behind her ears with both hands. She was dressed in her usual attire; black tights and an oversized gray sweater. "I just wanted to see how you were doing."

"You didn't have to come all the way out here," Kyle said. "You could have just sent me a text."

"I don't have your number, silly," she replied and gave him a soft smile. "Apparently, no one else in school does either."

Kyle shrugged.

"Is it okay if I hang out with you here for a bit before I walk back home?" Vanessa asked. "Or will that get in the way of your workout?"

"You walked here?"

"I walked to your house first. Your mom said you'd be here, so I walked here."

"Well, I appreciate you coming to check on me," Kyle said. "I'm okay."

"Okay, that's good," Vanessa said. "I just wanted to make sure in case you didn't want to come to school tomorrow."

"I'll be there tomorrow," Kyle said. "I can't really sit at home. That's why I'm here."

"Okay I'll see you tomorrow then," Vanessa said and started walking backwards toward the garage door. She gave him another smile and waved before turning around.

"Vanessa, wait," Kyle said. "I don't want you walking all the way home by yourself."

"I'll be fine. It's only about..." She looked down at her phone, "Four miles."

Kyle shook his head. "I guess it would have made sense for you to have my number."

"It would have. But what was I going to do? Wrestle you for it?" She smirked.

Kyle raised his eyebrows and almost smiled. "There is a bakery two blocks away. I didn't have breakfast, and I'm willing to bet you worked up an appetite while walking here."

"I sure did," Vanessa replied.

"Let's go get something there and I can walk you home after," Kyle said with a slight hesitation.

Vanessa lit up with a smile. "Okay!"

"Let me grab my stuff, lock up, and I'll meet you outside."

Kyle grabbed his bag with one hand, brushed his hair back with the other, and thought to himself, *Did I just ask her out on a date?*

He shut off all the lights and made his way out, under the garage doors.

"You didn't bring a sweater?" Vanessa asked as Kyle pulled down the rusty garage door with both hands.

"I actually jogged here," Kyle said. He bent down to lock the garage door.

"Okay, so we have something in common."

"Apparently, we do," Kyle said.

The two of them walked down the sidewalk side by side. It was a chilly spring afternoon, and then sun was beaming into their eyes, forcing them to squint.

After a few seconds of silence, Vanessa spoke up. "I saw the video online."

"I was hoping it wouldn't end up there," Kyle said with a sigh.

"It probably wouldn't have gone viral if Russel wasn't the son of Felix Coleman," Vanessa said.

"His Dad probably has it out for me," Kyle said. "And rightfully so."

"Why? Did you force Russel to wrestle?"

"No. He came to me looking for a place to train."

"Did you force him to do that crazy dive?"

"No. That was his idea but-"

"It was an accident, Kyle." Vanessa said.

"We are here," Kyle said. He opened the door and motioned for Vanessa to go in first.

"Kyle? A gentleman? Who would have known?" Vanessa asked.

Vanessa wanted a hot chocolate and a piece of cheesecake. Kyle usually stayed away from sweets, but the smell of fresh apple pie persuaded him to order a slice. Even the strictest dieters needed a cheat day, and he was no different.

Once the order was ready, he paid for it and met Vanessa at one of the small wooden tables opposite the displays of all the baked goods. He placed the tray down on the table and sat across from her.

"Thank you," Vanessa said as she gently grabbed the cup with two hands and brought it up to her lips for a tiny sip.

"How is it?" Kyle asked. He took a bite of his apple pie and chewed it slowly.

"Perfect for this weather," Vanessa said. She placed the cup to her left and shifted her attention to the cheesecake. "As I was saying before. It was an accident, and I hope you don't blame yourself."

"I should have talked him out of it," Kyle said. His eyes remained fixed on his slice of pie. "The move is very dangerous, and I knew it."

"Did you tell him that?"

"Of course. But he wanted to make an impression in his first match."

"I don't blame him for that. I wanted to do a whole bunch of flips during my first year on the Cheer Team."

"And did you?"

"No. The coach wouldn't go for it," Vanessa said with disappointment in her voice.

"You see?" Kyle said. "I should have talked him out of it. I should have never agreed to even team up with him. I'm nowhere near experienced enough to be on a team with someone so new to this. Maybe if it was someone in my place, they would have given him an idea for a different move."

"Hopefully he'll pull through," Vanessa said. "Apparently, his dad had him taken out of the Reign Memorial Hospital."

"Do you know why?"

"No one really knows. The rumor is that he is going to undergo some kind of experimental treatment."

"I need to go talk to his dad," Kyle said.

"I don't know if that's a good idea right now," Vanessa said with caution.

"It's the right thing to do," Kyle said. "The whole reason his son got into wrestling is because I told him about my friend Robert's school."

"You mean that garage?"

Kyle ignored her sarcastic comment.

"Vanessa, you had to see him," Kyle continued. "He's a natural athlete. He picked up the technique so quickly. It took me six months to get to where he was only at it for a few weeks."

"He'll pull through. I know it." Vanessa said. She reached across the table and put her hand on Kyle's. She almost regretted it right away, but Kyle didn't move his hand.

"I really hope you're right," Kyle replied and gave her hand a soft, hopeful squeeze.

———

"Sweetheart, I just don't think it's a good idea to get out there so soon," Janine said. "You're still dealing with what happened last week."

"Mom, I'm fine." Kyle insisted. He stuffed his gear into his bag and headed for the door.

"Make me a promise," Janine said. "No insane flips, please."

Kyle nodded with one foot out the door. "No flips. I promise."

Robert was parked on the curb. His red Ford Mustang had seen better days. There were signs of rust on the front bumper and scuffs on the passenger side door. He had purchased it fifteen years ago when he signed a rather sizable contract with a Japanese wrestling company. His run there didn't go as planned, and he was back in the States after only six months. He never got a call to come back. He managed to pay off the car with the money he had made there, as he gladly told anyone who was willing to listen.

"Hey kid," Robert said with a mouth full of his favorite meatball hero, which he was holding with both hands. "You're sure you're good to go for tonight?"

"I'm fine," Kyle said, trying not to sound annoyed.

"You'll be tagging with me today," Robert said. He stuffed the rest of the hero into his mouth before discarding the foil in the back seat. "Simple match. I'll be doing the honors."

Kyle nodded. He placed his bag on the back seat and put on his seatbelt. He wasn't fine despite what he was telling everyone, including himself. All he could think about was Russel. He was having a hard time falling asleep, and he would manage to finally doze off; he'd wake up from a nightmare where he had to relive Russel's accident over and over again.

It was an accident, he'd tell himself. *Injuries happen. It's part of the business.*

"Any news on Russel?" Robert asked as he pulled out of the parking spot.

"Nope," Kyle replied. "I tried to go speak to his Dad a couple of days ago. They wouldn't let me into the building."

"I can't imagine what his father is feeling right now," Robert said. "I've seen many wrestlers get hurt. A torn ACL, maybe a dislocated shoulder. Never anything like this."

"I know," Kyle said.

"There are rumors that Mr. Coleman is going to try some experimental treatments on his son," Robert said. The car jerked as he picked up speed to merge onto the highway. "With his resources, I don't think he is going to stop until his son is back on his feet."

"I wish there was something I could do to help," Kyle said.

"I think, at this point, you just have to let the doctors do their work," Robert said. His eyes were fixed on the road. "I'm sure you've heard it from everyone multiple times, but I'm going to say it again. It wasn't your fault. I've spent enough time training that kid to know that once he sets his mind to something, there is no turning back. That's why he took to wrestling so quickly."

"He was a natural," Kyle said. "In the back of my mind, I had no doubt that he could have pulled off that move."

"He was fully capable of it."

"I wish I would have just said no to him when he asked me to train him."

"We both meant well," Robert said. "This is going to stay with us for a long time. We are going to have to learn to live with it."

Kyle rolled down the window and focused his attention on the hustle and bustle of the highway.

They drove the rest of the way in silence.

———

Felix was always a big supporter of automation. He believed machines running completely on autopilot was the future. What he never expected was that he would run on autopilot.

It had been a week since his son's accident. He didn't miss a day of work. He attended every meeting, responded to every email, and returned all of his phone calls. He did all of those things in a fog, as if he was watching himself run his company from a distance.

Felix stepped out of his office and made his way down the hall towards the elevator. For the first time, he didn't know everyone in the building by name. People said hello to him, and he would say hello back, but he had no idea who most of those people were. This was a result of Mr. Okada's involvement. He came on as a partner and brought his operations over to the Coleman Tech building.

The elevator doors hissed open before Felix had a chance to press a button. A group of young men carrying their laptops stepped out, talking and laughing with each other. When they saw Felix, all of that came to a halt. They said hello and quickly exited the elevator. Felix stepped in and pressed the button for the basement.

Once the elevator stopped, Felix stepped out and made a sharp left. He walked to the very end of the hall with his key card in hand. The lock mechanism lit up in green as soon as he approached it, and the doors slid open. He entered a dark room with only one source of light in the center. It was a blue light emanating from a floor ceiling cylinder shaped tank. Inside was Russel's floating body. He had a breathing device that covered his nose and mouth, as well as, a few sensors on his forehead, neck and chest.

Felix put his left hand on the glass. "We'll be together soon, son. I promise."

"You will be together. Not sure if soon is the right word."

"Who is there?" Felix asked. He tried to follow the voice but saw no one in the darkness.

"It's me Mr. Coleman." Mr. Okada said and stepped into the light.

'"What are you doing here in the dark?" Felix asked.

"I had just finished adjusting your son's settings," Mr. Okada said. "As I've told you before, we've never tried a procedure on this scale before."

"You never told me where this technology came from," Felix said. "There is no way you made these kinds of leaps and bounds on your own in such a short time."

"You are even smarter than most people give you credit for." Mr. Okada said with a smirk. "You are correct. I had help from an outside source."

"I would be aware if anyone had anything like this in development anywhere in the world," Felix said. His gaze remained fixed on his son's floating body.

"The creators of this technology are, how would I say this?" Mr. Okada paused. "Not from around here."

"Where are they from then?"

"You wouldn't believe it."

"Try me."

Mr. Okada clasped his hands behind his back and circled Russel's tank. "A few months ago, I was cast out by my business partners because I was doing research that made them feel uneasy. I was exploring interdimensional travel."

Felix looked over and raised his eyebrows.

"They didn't believe it at first either," Mr. Okada continued. "They thought I was losing my mind until one day, I opened a portal into another dimension and made contact with a scientist who was searching for a way to connect with us. I saw it as a huge discovery and an amazing business opportunity. They have the technology we can only dream of. My partners were scared. They locked me out of my lab, destroyed all my research, and set me back a few months."

"You were right. I wouldn't have believed you," Felix said. "But this tech here is like nothing I've ever seen before. I take it you were able to reconnect with this other dimension?"

"I was able to do much more than that," Mr. Okada said. "I established a partnership with them. Or should I say we did?"

Felix had an uneasy feeling in the pit of his stomach. He shifted his attention to his son and reminded himself that everything he would do from here on out would be done to create a safer world for his son to live in, no matter when he'd fully recover.

———

The ring was always Kyle's escape from reality, and this night was no different. He was laser focused on every move, he effortlessly bounced off the ropes, and his timing was impeccable. He and Robert were booked to lose the match, but they put on quite a show.

After the match, most of the other wrestlers came up to Kyle in the locker room and inquired about Russel. He received a few pep talks. Most of them reiterated what Robert and his mom had been telling him all week. Accidents happen, and it wasn't his fault.

Kyle nodded along and didn't say much.

The locker room began to empty out when Robert walked over. "Hey kid, we are doing a little meet and greet at the bar across the street. Meet me there after you change."

"Okay," Kyle said.

Robert grabbed his bag and rushed everyone out of the locker room.

Kyle closed his eyes and massaged the bridge of his nose. Once the show came to an end, the adrenaline began to leave Kyle's body. Reality set in once again, and Kyle's mind drifted back towards Russel.

Kyle stood up and turned towards his locker. He began putting the sweaty clothes into his bag when a shadowy figure crept into the locker room unannounced.

Kyle never got to lay his eyes on the visitor.

The last thing he felt was a stinging sensation in his neck before everything went dark.

SIX

20 Years Later…

Terry Wilson was only three years old when the world changed. He never knew the world before the toxin was released. Most people in their early twenties had no idea anything was wrong. They grew up in a world that didn't know war, didn't know any conflict at all. Hunger was something they only read about in text books, and violence could only be seen in decade old movies.

The world Terry grew up in operated at a controlled speed. Everyone drove the speed limit, and walked down the street with extreme caution; no one ever littered or even jay walked. The very few people that did, disappeared without a trace. Few returned, but no one would ever say where they were taken. No one ever confronted anyone because everyone was afraid of confrontation.

They were also afraid of the androids that patrolled the streets.

Terry stood on one of the busiest corners in Reign. A large black hood concealed his face, showing only the tips of his evenly parted, pencil straight hair. His green eyes darted from one side of the street to the other. He was surrounded by dozens of pedestrians who walked down the immaculately clean streets of Reign.

Terry was waiting for an opening. He waited for the street to be clear of the androids. Their perfectly shaved heads and sleek, skin tight, dark blue uniforms patrolled the streets. If there was even a sign of any commotion, they'd snatch the perpetrators and take them in for a few tests. No one knew exactly what the tests were, but of the few people that came back, none could remember what was done to them.

There were only two androids on the street. Terry reached into the pocket of his jacket and retrieved a wire. He held it hidden in his right hand and prowled towards the information terminal on the side of the Coleman Tech security tower.

He took one last glance before turning around and plugging his wire into the side of the terminal. He unzipped his jacket and revealed a small tablet. With his free hand, he reached up towards his left ear and clicked the small communication device in his ear.

"Control. I'm in."

"Excellent Terry," replied a deep, familiar voice on the other end. "There are no androids in your immediate vicinity. You have three minutes and thirty-six seconds to locate the subject."

Terry didn't waste time responding. He was busy trying to bypass the firewall and obtain the information that he needed to move to the next step of his mission.

"Two minutes fifty seconds," Control said.

Terry felt the cold sweat on his palms as he continued to punch away at the vibrating keyboard on the screen of his tablet. His heart was beating harder than it ever had before. He had been exposed to the toxin when he was in grade school. After years of toxin therapy, this was the riskiest mission yet. It was also the most important one.

"One minute."

"I know," Terry mumbled under his breath.

He was close, and he knew it. He didn't know if one minute would be enough.

"Thirty seconds."

"Come on," Terry said. He watched the loading bar creep up from thirty percent to sixty-seven. "Almost there."

"Ten seconds."

"It's at ninety percent," Terry said. "I just need another few seconds."

"You are now within the patrol perimeter on an android unit," said Control. "Terrance, you have to go. Now!"

"Done!" Terry snatched the wire out of the panel and shoved the tablet back into his pocket. He spotted the android out of the corner of his eye and took off in the opposite direction.

"He is on to you Terry," Control said.

"I'm going to make a run for it," Terry said nervously.

"Not yet, Terry," Control said slowly. "I'm sending Number Two. He'll create a distraction and give you a chance to make it back to base."

"Okay," Terry said. "How far is he?"

"Less than a minute away," Control said.

Terry fought the urge to turn around and check how far off the android was. He walked at a steady pace. If he attempted to walk faster than the people around him, it would immediately give him away.

"I wish I didn't need Number Two," Terry said.

"One day you won't, Terry," Control said.

Terry listened for the familiar sound of Number Two's motorcycle. He could hear a distant buzzing in the distance. As the sound got louder, he prepared to run. It was going to be a challenge for him as the street became unusually crowded. Terry tried to push through slowly without attracting attention.

"He is close by," Control said. "I sent the rendezvous coordinates to the tablet."

People scurried away as soon as the bike screeched to a halt. Number Two leaped into the air and tackled the android to the ground.

"Terry! Run!" Control yelled into the ear piece.

Terry took out the tablet and took off.

"The door directly ahead across the street should be unlocked," Control said. "Get in there and wait for Number Two."

Terry picked up the pace and sprinted for the door.

Tires screeched as Number Two used his bike to get between Terry and the Android. He hopped off his bike and ditched his jacket revealing a slick, black metallic armor that covered him from the neck down. He kept his helmet on and engaged the Android in hand-to-hand combat.

The street was suddenly clear, with Number Two wrestling the android to the ground only a few yards away from Terry. Terry burst through the door, locked it behind him and ran up a short flight of stairs to the window.

He peered through an old, dusty curtain and was able to see the struggle between Number Two and his adversary. In the few seconds that it took Terry to get to the window, the android gained the upper hand. Number Two was on the ground with his motorcycle helmet still on his head. He was dodging punches from the android. Even from a distance, Terry could see the dents in the cement from the android's punches. Number Two managed to squirm out of the way and quickly regained his footing. He reached across his body and unzipped a pocket on his right arm. Terry knew exactly what Number Two was doing. He was going to try to paralyze the android temporarily with a jolt of strong electric current. The only problem was that he needed to get close to the android's neck and the android was at least a foot taller than him.

Terry chewed on his index finger nail as he watched Number Two stumble away from the android. Terry knew the right thing to do would be to go out there and help, but he was completely frozen in fear. The only part of his body capable of motion was the trembling hand that was holding the curtain.

Number Two was able to put some distance between himself and the android before lunging at him and delivering a shock to his neck. Terry watched as the android stumbled backwards and froze in place seconds later. Number Two jumped onto his bike.

"Terry, get ready to move," Control said. "There are six more androids incoming."

Terry rubbed his hands together and took a deep breath. He stood up slowly and made his way downstairs. Number Two was waiting for him outside. Terry jumped onto the back seat of the bike and grabbed on to Number Two.

"You got what you came for?" Number Two asked. His voice was barely audible through the helmet.

"I did."

"Good. Hold on tight."

Number Two revved the engine, and the two of them were gone before reinforcements arrived.

―――――

Number Two brought his Bike to a complete halt a few yards inside of a cave about two miles away from the City of Reign. Terry hopped off the bike and waited for a jolt. A sudden movement shook the floor of the cave as Number Two, and Terry felt the floor of the cave begin to descend. It moved slowly, but Terry held on to the bike just in case.

Once they were a few yards below the surface, an almost identical platform covered their trail above them. When the platform they were standing on came to a complete stop, Terry and Number Two found themselves in the middle of the control room. All around them were countless monitors with operators sitting behind each one. Everyone worked together to perform important functions that ensured the location of the cave remained a secret.

"It feels good to be back."

"It really does, Number Two," Terry said as he climbed off the bike.

"You don't have to use code names down here," said the man known as Control out in the field. Underground, he simply went by Alex. "You can call him Russel."

Alex took a few steps and joined the others on the platform.

"Sorry, Alex," Terry said. "You know I get rattled during these missions."

"No need to apologize," Alex said. His voice echoed thanks to the high ceilings of the control room.

"You're the only skilled programmer that's willing to go on these missions," Russel said. "Also, without you, Alex would never have found me."

Terry shrugged off the compliment.

Alex gave him a warm smile that accentuated the wrinkles around his eyes, which looked even bigger behind his perfectly circle rimmed glasses. His gray hair was neatly brushed to the side. He wore the standard olive green uniform suit which was identical to everyone else's in the room.

"We should see what Terry was able to pull from that terminal," Russel said.

Alex nodded and motioned for the young men to follow him to his office next door to the control room. They walked past three long rows of computers, most of which were occupied by the security staff monitoring the surrounding areas for potential threats. Once Terry made it through the door, he walked straight to Alex's computer and plugged in the USB, which was holding the information that he had collected.

The majority of the office wall space was taken up with blueprints of different buildings and maps of Reign and the surrounding areas. Alex took his place behind his desk once Terry was done. Russel joined Terry on the two chairs that were facing Alex.

"Let's see what we have here," Alex said as he opened the file.

Both Terry and Russel had their gaze fixed on Alex. Neither one of them said a word.

"I think we've got his location," Alex said and nodded in approval.

"Yes! Finally!" Russel said and shook his fists in front of himself. He reached over with his right hand and gave Terry a fist bump. "Great job, Terry! This is really going to help our cause."

"I hope so. I wish there was more I could do." Terry said, and shrugged again,

"We need someone quick and agile, right?" Russel asked. "Someone who can go on missions with me and has never been exposed to the toxin? Someone that can tussle with an android when required."

"Yes," Alex said. "However, we want to avoid tussles with any androids. I don't need to remind you how many of our people have tried to go toe to toe with those things never to be seen again. Or worse."

Russel reeled himself in and sat down. "I know Alex. I've been here for two years, and I've seen what the androids can do."

"I've been here for twenty, and I have yet to see things start moving in the right direction," Alex said.

"What's the plan moving forwards?" Terry asked.

"We need to go get this kid," Alex said. "We need to bring him back here and evaluate his mental and physical condition. Don't discount the fact that he's been on ice for almost two decades."

"I was on ice almost as long," Russel said. "I came out just fine."

"I was there when they transferred you in," Alex said. "Your Dad made sure you were set up properly and well taken care of. He monitored your progress every day until he disappeared. Nobody monitored the others."

"The others?" Terry asked. "How many were there?"

"I'm not sure," Alex said in a somber tone. "My last few months in Coleman Tech were hectic. It's hard to remember everything that happened after Felix disappeared, leaving Okada in charge."

"We shouldn't waste any more time then," Russel said.

"Let me start by saying this isn't going to be easy," Alex said while looking at his screen. "And you're going to have to do this mission alone."

"That's fine with me."

"He is being held in a small, but highly guarded facility," Alex began. "There are five androids on guard duty there. Now, these are not the regular street patrolling units. These second-generation units. There is no other way for me to put this; if you try to take them on, they will kill you. Your best bet is to outrun them, which you should still be able to do by my calculations."

Terry looked over at Russel, who was clearly doing his best to hide his fear. Terry was absolutely terrified of androids, but he was also envious of Russel's ability to control his fear.

"There has to be a weakness," Terry said after a brief pause.

"None that we know of so far," Terry intervened. "Since these units aren't on patrol, we haven't been able to analyze them very closely. The only thing we do know is that the eclectic currents will not work on them."

"They are also faster and stronger than the street patrollers," Alex added.

"It sounds like a challenge," Russel said. "But we don't really have a choice here."

Terry and Alex both nodded in agreement.

"Terry, get me the best armor we have," Russel said. "I'm going to get him. Then we are going after Coleman Tech with everything we've got."

———

Armors were Terry's specialty, and he had his best one ready for Russel less than thirty minutes after their meeting with Alex. The two of them met up down the hall from Alex's office, right outside of Terry's daytime workshop.

"It may take some getting used to, but it'll do the job." Terry handed a bulky briefcase over to Russel.

"I'm sure it will," Russel said. "There aren't too many people who would have been able to do what you did out there today."

"Don't Russel," Terry said with a serious look on his face. "I don't want to hear it. All I did was get some codes. You had to come to save me because I'm still too afraid to confront an android on my own."

"It's not your fault you-"

"All of this training that I do. All of our sparring sessions. What's the point of it all if I'm too scared to put any of it to use?" Russel asked.

"I'm not going to sugar coat anything for you," Russel said. "I don't know when the toxin will wear off. What I do know is that when it's time to step up, I believe that you will."

"How can you know?"

"Certain things a toxin can't take away from you," Russel said. He gave Terry a light punch in the chest with his one free hand. "You've got heart. At your core, you're a brave kid."

Terry nodded, but his expression remained unchanged. "Good luck out there. I hope you find who you're looking for."

"Thank you," Terry said. He lifted up the briefcase. "And thanks for this too."

"Where do you think you're going?"

Russel and Terry turned around and spotted Alex squeezing past a few people in the tight hallway.

"I'm going to suit up for the next mission," Russel said.

"You just came back from a mission," Alex said. "You need to check in with Charlotte for a medical observation."

"Alex, we don't have time for that," Russel insisted.

Alex gave him a stern look. "I don't remember putting this up for debate."

"Fine." Russel sighed as he brushed past Alex and continued down the hall towards the Medical Station.

The halls had low ceilings and were barely wide enough for two people to walk side by side. There were very strict emergency procedure drills every two weeks to ensure that everyone is able to get to the exits in an orderly fashion. If panic were to take hold in one of these halls, it would put all ninety residents of the underground complex in danger.

Russel walked up to the sliding doors at the end of the hall and watched as they slid open for him. He stepped into the best lit room in the entire underground complex and gave his eyes a few seconds to adjust.

"Russel, I'll be right with you!" The complex doctor, Charlotte called out from behind one of the dividers.

"Okay, I'll wait out here," Russel replied.

"No, you go ahead into room three," Charlotte said before Russel had a chance to sit on the bench along the back wall. "Just sign in first, please."

Russel walked up to the desk on his right and signed his name on the clipboard. Then, he proceeded to room three.

The room was a very loose description of an area that was split away from the rest of the office by a thin curtain. Russel sat in the patient chair and enjoyed the relative silence. All he could hear was Charlotte shuffling around a few feet away and the steady buzzing of the lights above.

"Okay, let's get started, shall we?" Charlotte asked as she burst through the curtain. A slender woman in her mid-twenties, her hair was in a neat, thick braid, and it ran all the way down her back. She was wearing a white shirt, and matching lab coat and had a pair of thin, rimless glasses that did little to hide the bags under her eyes.

Russel watched her as she pulled up his chart on her tablet. "When was the last time you had a day off, Charlotte?"

"I haven't had a day off in quite some time," Charlotte admitted without looking up. "Between the toxin treatments, the checkups, and general treatments, there isn't a lot of time left in the day."

"I see," Russel said. "I can talk to Alex. See if we can focus on bringing you some help from the surface."

"That would be helpful," Charlotte said. She placed the tablet down. "But I'll take being busy all day here than living in a dream world up there."

"I agree with you on that," Russel said.

"Let's have a look at you. Alex told me you mixed it up with another android up there."

"I did," Russel said. "It was nothing serious."

"Of course not," Charlotte said unamused. "Yet somehow you're the only one that's ever faced an android and lived to talk about it."

"To be fair, the ones before me tried to put up a fight, but they were at a huge disadvantage" Russel said. "I was never exposed to that toxin and my main purpose out there is to make sure that no one else gets taken."

A look of sadness flashed across Charlotte's face. Her father was one of the first scouts after the underground complex was established. He went on a routine mission to the surface five years earlier and never came back. "Lean back in the chair. I'm going to do a quick scan to make sure you're good to go back up there."

Russel did as he was told. Charlotte stepped out behind the curtain and returned as soon as the scan was completed. She pulled up the images on her tablet and studied them without saying a word.

"Everything okay?" Russel asked.

"Alex said you were in a pretty serious fight this time," Charlotte said. Her eyes remained fixed on the tablet.

"That's right."

"When was that exactly?

"About three hours ago."

"This can't be right then," Charlotte said and looked at Russel.

"What's wrong?" Russel asked.

"I can't definitively say that something is wrong," Charlotte said. "It's just that the bruises on your hip, shoulders, and elbows look like they are halfway through the healing process."

"Isn't that a good thing?"

"It's just that I can't explain how you manage to heal so quickly," Charlotte said.

Russel looked at her and shrugged. "I can't explain it either. I feel fine, though."

I'm going to take a closer look at this later," Charlotte said. "You're free to go. I sent the clearance over to Alex."

"Thank you, Charlotte," Russel said and hopped out of the chair. "I'm most likely bringing in a new recruit later on today."

"Alex told me to have two treatment areas ready to go," Charlotte said. "I heard the mission is quite dangerous. Something about a new model of androids."

"Yes," Russel said as he moved the curtain aside. "The person I'm going after is going to be a difference maker. I know it."

———

Kyle felt a soft nudge on his shoulder as he rolled over to the other side to hopefully continue sleeping.

"Honey, you've slept for ten hours. It's time to get up."

"I thought when I moved out of my mom's house, I'd get to sleep in for as long as I wanted," Kyle said without opening his eyes.

"All of that went out the window when you decided to marry me," Vanessa said and hit him with a pillow.

"Okay, I'm up, I'm up." Kyle opened one eye and looked at Vanessa.

"You know, I'm really glad Kevin didn't inherit your sleeping abilities," she said.

"I don't remember you saying things like that when you want to sleep in," Kyle stood up and put his arms out for a stretch. "Where is Kevin anyway?"

"He's downstairs with you mom," Vanessa said. "Were you in another hardcore match on this past tour? Every time you're in one of these matches, it takes a few days for my functioning husband to return."

"No hardcore matches this time around," Kyle said as he pulled the covers over the bed. "You know I stopped taking chair shots almost ten years ago."

"I'm glad you came to your senses about that sooner than later," Vanessa said. She looped around the bed and gave Kyle a soft kiss on the cheek. "Get dressed. Your mom and Kevin are waiting for you to have breakfast."

Kyle walked up to the drawer and pulled it open. He grabbed a short sleeve shirt, but before he could pull it over his head, he caught a glimpse of himself in the mirror that hung on their door. He looked himself up and down and slowly brought his fist up to his chest, flexing his bicep and admiring his chiseled physique.

I'm in great shape, but I can hardly remember what I did to look like this.

He shook his head and pulled the shirt over his head. He finished getting dressed, brushed his teeth and made his way downstairs. "Mom, good to see you bright and early on Saturday morning."

Janine was on the couch opposite the staircase with her grandson on her lap. "You and I have always had different interpretations of bright and early, dear."

"Daddy! You're awake!" Kevin hopped off Janine's lap and ran over to hug Kyle.

"That's right buddy," Kyle replied and scooped his son up off the floor with two hands. "And I'm all yours for the rest of the day."

Kevin smiled and wrapped his arms around Kyle. "I'm so excited to go to the zoo!"

"Me too," Kyle said, doing his best to match his son's youthful enthusiasm.

Vanessa emerged from the kitchen. "Everyone ready? Grandpa Joe is waiting in the car."

"Grandpa?" Kyle asked with a puzzled look on his face.

"Yes," Vanessa said. "Your dad is here. He always drives to the zoo."

Kyle took his eyes off of his wife and stared at the floor. He knew Vanessa was not one to joke about something like this. He thought hard until a stream of memories rushed back into his head as if they were being held back by a dam that had finally burst. He remembered his father coming back into their lives around the time he graduated High School. It took a few months, but he changed. No more drinking, smoking, not even an occasional argument with his mom. He began to attend Kyle's wrestling shows and all of Timmy's events at school. He remembered how happy his dad was when Kevin was born. He gave Kyle a hug tighter than any bear hug he had ever received in the ring.

"Honey," Vanessa said. "Are you sure you're okay?"

"Yeah. I'm fine," Kyle said and forced a smile. "Let's not keep grandpa waiting."

Janine and Vanessa headed for the door.

Kevin took Kyle's hand and led him towards the door as well. "Come on, Dad! Grandpa said he's buying ice cream for everyone if we get there early."

SEVEN

Russel checked the map on his motorcycle and convinced himself
that he had arrived at the right place. He was looking at a small
brick building. It was two stories tall and had its windows covered. If
there was a light on in there nobody was going to be able to see it. The
only light outside of the building was coming from the full moon
above.

Russel hopped off the motorcycle in one motion and landed with
his feet facing the steel door. He approached the entrance watching his
step, in case there were any alarms outside of the building. Luckily,
there were none and he proceeded to test the door.

Locked. Okay, that was to be expected.

He glanced down at his utility belt. A collaborative addition from
Terry and Alex to the sleek black armor. Russel reached into the small
opening above his left hip and retrieved a small circular device. Alex
claimed there was no door that the device wouldn't be able to unlock.
He clipped the device onto the door and stepped back. He listened for
a quiet ticking. A few seconds later, the panel on the door lit up in
green and Russel opened the door with extreme caution.

All clear. Okay, this is a good start for me.

He clicked a few buttons on his watch and turned on the android proximity device. It wasn't a perfect system, but it would alert him if there was an android close by. He scanned the area with his eyes first, and when he didn't detect any movement, he shifted his gaze down to the watch. There were four red dots on different sides of the building. They were moving very slowly. Russel pushed a few more buttons and the watch produced a path to the room that was holding the person he was after.

Russel made his way down a pitch-black hallway. As with most android controlled facilities, there was no reason to have lights. The androids were fully capable of seeing in the dark. Unfortunately, Russel did not have that ability. He reached back into his utility belt and slid out a thin pair of night vision goggles. He put them on, trying to make as little noise as possible and spotted a staircase up ahead. He checked his watch once again, made sure there were no androids close by and sprinted for the stairs. He made his way up the stairs and down another hallway before coming to a complete stop.

I guess this is where my luck ran out, Russel thought as he pinned his back against the wall. There was a pair of androids walking past the very door that led to his target's location.

Okay, let's see what else they've got in this belt for me today.

Russel began to search the pockets one by one until he came across a small projector with tiny wheels on the bottom. There was a note next to one of the tires that read; *the watch is the controller.* Russel placed the projector on the floor and followed the instructions to activate his watch. He gave the projector a quick test run by his feet before sending full speed ahead right past the androids who had their back turned to Russel.

Once the projector was at the far end of the hall Russel pressed the button for the projection, and suddenly, there were three people running down the hall in front of the android. This caused the androids to take off running at an alarming speed. It also gave Russel the opening he needed to get inside the holding chamber. He quickly programmed the projector to keep rolling and made a dash for the door, which was once again locked. He reached into the same pocket and was delighted to find another lock override chip. He placed it on the door but did not step away this time. The door slid open, and blue light emanated from six floor to ceiling cylinders. Each one was about six feet apart and had a person floating in it with nothing but an oxygen mask and a few sensors on their head and torso.

Russel scurried in, still attempting to make as little noise as possible. He moved from one cylinder to another. He clicked the light on his shoulder and took pictures of the people inside the holding pods, just in case. He spotted exactly who he was looking for in the fifth pod. His body was pale with hair floating in different directions, but Russel was convinced that Terry's information was correct. He pushed the release button on the side of the cylinder and watched as the water began to drain. It wasn't Russel's first release procedure, but it was definitely the highest risk one to date.

Just as the last of the water drained from the cylinder, Russel saw a large shadow emerging from the entrance. He turned just in time to see an android step in and rush right at him.

Kevin ran ahead to check out his favorite animal; the lion. Vanessa and Jeanine stayed close behind while Kyle and his dad trailed a few feet behind them.

"Is everything okay, son?"

"Yeah," Kyle said without hesitation. "I just have a very strange feeling that all of this is a dream."

"How is that possible?" Joe asked. "This is your life. You've got everything you ever wanted."

"That's exactly it." Kyle stopped and looked at his dad. "I've always wanted all of this. A family, a successful wrestling career, a nice house, and it may be odd for you to hear this but I've always wanted a close relationship with you. One just like this."

"You deserve it all," Joe said. "I'm very proud of you son. Always have been and always will be."

Kyle!

"Did you hear that, dad?"

"Hear what?" Joe asked. He looked at his son and then turned around to look behind them.

Kyle took a few steps forward and looked around. He saw the paths that led to different animal exhibits, the benches and neatly trimmed bushes along those paths. He saw the other people, and everyone looked happy. The sun was shining, and only a few yards ahead, he saw his son, along with his wife and mother, admiring the lions behind the glass.

"Kyle," Joe said as he walked up to his son. "Are you sure you're alright?"

Kyle looked at his father, and he could tell that he was scaring him by the look on his face. "I feel like this is all a dream, dad. I can't explain it, but I feel like I'm about to wake up."

"Let's take a seat," Joe said and motioned toward a bench on the opposite side of the path.

"No!" Kyle snapped. "There is no time! I need to get to Kevin!"

"Kyle!" Joe called, but it was too late. His son took off running, and there was no catching up to him.

Kyle pushed past a few people who were on the way to the lion exhibit, but managed to slow down as he approached Vanessa and his mom.

"Honey, are you okay?" Vanessa asked. "Why are you breathing so heavy?"

"I don't have much time," Kyle said and hugged his wife tightly. He proceeded to hug his mother before making his way towards Kevin. The four-year-old boy was completely oblivious to what was going on behind him. He was mesmerized by the lions. "Kevin, buddy?"

The boy turned around. "Yes, Dad?"

Kyle!

Kyle flinched and looked to each side of him in hopes of seeing who was calling his name. There were people all around him but everyone was engaged with their friends and families.

"Kevin, listen to me." Kyle got on his knees and took his son by the shoulders. "Daddy has to go now."

"Where?" Kevin asked, unable to hide his disappointment. "You just came back last night."

"I know son," Kyle said. "I can't explain what's going on, but I want you to know that I love you."

"I love you too Daddy," Kevin said with tears streaming down his face.

KYLE!

Kyle closed his eyes, hoping the voice in his head would go away.

When he opened his eyes, everyone was gone. He was alone in pitch-black darkness.

The only thing that remained was the voice in his head.

Kyle! Wake up!

———

His eye lids felt like they weighed a ton, but Kyle knew he had to force them open. As he tried to blink himself out of the sleepy state, he realized that he was hot and cold at the same time. His body felt numb, but the feeling was slowly coming back into his joints, limbs, and finally, his fingers and toes. He had the urge to roll out of bed when he suddenly became dizzy as he realized he was standing up and that he was surrounded by glass. Kyle tried to lift his arms to rub his eyes and move his hair away from his face when the glass began to lift up, leaving him with nothing to hold on to.

Kyle flopped forward. He attempted to break his fall with his forearms but failed miserably and felt his face bounce off the floor. He became even more disoriented than before as he watched two pairs of feet, one pair significantly bigger than the other, go back and forth.

"Kyle! Can you hear me?"

Kyle could hear someone calling to him. The voice was familiar, but there was a lot of background noise, and everything sounded muffled.

A familiar face ran up to Kyle. He tried to remember who it was but his head felt like it became even heavier when he tried to think.

"Kyle! It's Russel! I know you're confused. Your legs probably feel like jelly, but we have to get out of here!"

Russel, Kyle thought as he tried to push himself up off the floor. *I know that name.*

Russel disappeared into a thick cloud of smoke only to pop on the other side of Kyle a few seconds later.

"We don't have much time," Russel said. He grabbed Kyle's right arm and swung it over his shoulder. "Reinforcements will be here any minute."

Kyle did his best not to slow Russel down as the two of them trotted out of the smoky room and down what seemed to be a never-ending set of stairs. Kyle's legs indeed felt like jelly, but once they made it down to what he hoped was the first floor, he was able to support himself a bit more.

"Just a little further," Russel said. He picked up the pace and kicked the door open.

"Where are we?" Kyle asked as soon as they stepped outside. "What's going on?"

"I'll explain everything soon," Russel said. "Lean on my bike for a second."

Kyle did as he was told. He had no other choice. He was convinced that if he let go of the bike, he would collapse on the floor, and he wasn't sure he'd be able to make it back to his feet this time.

"Put this on quick!" Russel said. He handed Kyle a garment that resembled a huge robe.

It was at this moment that Kyle realized he was freezing and completely naked. He threw the robe over his shoulders with some help from Russel, who proceeded to pick him up by the waist and place him on the back part of the motorcycle.

"They're gaining on us," Russel said. He hopped on to the bike and revved the engine. "I know this sounds like a lot to ask for in your current state, but I need you to hold on tight."

Kyle grabbed onto Russel and felt a huge jolt followed by a strong wind as they raced through a bumpy path through the woods. He felt dizzy all over again and opted to close his eyes, but not fall asleep. Whatever they were running away from, he did not want it to catch him in this weakened and confused state.

———

Every muscle and tendon in his body felt as if it had a needle poking it every time Kyle tried to move. Even blinking hurt, but he needed to know where he was. He attempted to sit up and was quickly convinced to lay back down by the shooting pain in his neck and back.

"Easy there Kyle," said a young woman in a white lab coat. She approached the bed and made sure he laid back down slower than he attempted to sit up.

"Who are you?" he murmured. "And where am I? Where is Vanessa?"

"My name is Charlotte," the young woman responded with a warm smile. "You're in a safe place. We are just running some tests to see how we can get you back on your feet."

Still suffering from the worst headache he'd ever experienced, Kyle closed his eyes and drifted back to sleep.

Charlotte placed her hand on his forehead. He had been running quite a fever when Russel brought him in, but it had subsided since then. She glanced at her newest patient one more time, and closed the curtain separating him from her most frequent visitor.

"How's he doing?" Russel asked. He was laying down but sat up quickly when Charlotte entered.

"He is doing okay, all things considered," Charlotte said. She walked over to the small desk next to Russel's bed and picked up a clipboard with the list of his latest injuries.

"How long before he can join me on a mission?"

"It's hard to tell. He has been in stasis for a while and it doesn't seem like he was as well taken care of as you were," Charlotte said and glanced over at Russel's bandaged torso and right arm. "You are both lucky to have made it back here."

"It was a standard mission." Russel shrugged.

"I'll tell you what's not standard," Charlotte said as she lifted up a pair of X-Rays and examined them in the light. "Your injuries."

"These weren't the standard androids I'm used to. It took a few smoke grenades and a lot of luck to make it out of there."

"I see three broken ribs, a tiny fracture in your forearm, not to mention a concussion and more bruises than I care to count," Charlotte said. She placed the clipboard, along with the X-Rays, down on the desk and shifted her gaze over to Russel.

"Three broken ribs," he said. "That explains the sharp pain I feel every time I take a deep breath."

"Yes." Charlotte said and took his injured forearm with both hands. She began to gently press down on the area that was fractured. "Just as I suspected. The fracture has completely healed, and it's only been four hours."

"That can't be," Russel smirked. "Fractures can't heal that quickly."

"You're right. They shouldn't."

"Maybe the X-Ray machine is malfunctioning."

"No. The machine is just fine," Charlotte said. She pushed her glasses back up the bridge of her nose. "This isn't the first time that I've seen an injury heal at an accelerated rate on you."

"Have you shared this information with anyone?"

"I haven't said anything to anyone. I'd never seen anything like this before and I wanted to do some research before jumping to any conclusions," Charlotte said.

"Did you find anything out?" Russel asked. He slowly took the bandages off of his arm and examined it.

"There isn't anything wrong with you," Charlotte said. Her gaze was fixed on his unbandaged arm, which showed no signs of any injury. Even the bruises had subsided. "I believe that whatever was used to heal your body in that tank for twenty years, it altered your body's healing capabilities."

"I see." Russel leaned back and took a deep breath. "Have you seen this happen to any of the other people we've rescued from the tanks?"

"No," Charlotte said. "Almost all of them were exposed to the toxin, so they never put themselves in a situation where they could be injured."

Russel nodded. "Do you think Kyle has that same healing ability?"

"It's too soon to tell," Charlotte said and made her way towards the foot of the bed. "I'm going to keep a close eye on him."

"I'm probably going to get out of here sooner than later," Russel said and looked down at his right arm. "Let me know when he wakes up. I'm sure he'll have more questions, and it'll be good for him to hear some answers from a familiar face."

"Of course," Charlotte said. "Get some rest. You're not completely healed yet."

After Charlotte left the room, Russel's mind began to wonder. He never really suffered any serious injuries as a kid. He never had any broken bones or tears in any ligaments.

Could it be possible that I've always had this ability?

There was no way to be sure.

Russel felt his ribs with his fingers. They still felt tender, but he no longer felt any pain while breathing. There could have been a worse side effect, so he decided not to stress over it.

Besides, there were other things to worry about. The new model of androids wasn't exactly a welcome addition to the number of threats that Russel was already facing every time he went above ground. He sat up once again and looked around the room for his armor. It was nowhere to be seen.

Terry got his hands on it, Russel told himself.

Terry was in charge of examining the footage that was recorded by the armor while Russel was on the surface. He and Alex worked diligently to create tools and weapons to both combat the androids when necessary and develop scrambling technology to keep them from following Russel back to the base.

Alex had a contingency plan for every situation. Russel was convinced that he had one just in case the androids ever discovered their location. He hoped that day would never come, but if it did, Russel was sure that he would be the first line of defense.

He couldn't help himself. He felt nearly invincible after finding out that he had accelerated healing abilities.

———

Kyle woke up drenched in what he hoped was his own sweat. His breathing was heavy and uneven, but the pain he felt earlier had subsided. He took inventory of his surroundings and came to the conclusion that he was in a hospital.

How did I get here?

He sat up straight in his bed and rubbed his temple. He tried to think back to the last thing he could recall. There was running through a dark hallway with a familiar face. He closed his eyes and tried hard to remember.

Russel! He was saving from whatever that place was.

Kyle took a deep breath and planted his feet on the floor. He was dressed in a hospital gown. He couldn't remember what he was wearing prior to his arrival, but he didn't see any clothes on his bed or the chairs perpendicular to the bed. He scanned the room for anything that might give him a clue about where he was. He spotted a clipboard on the desk right next to his bed.

He grabbed it and started reading through it. Most of it was standard information, such as his name, age, and weight. It wasn't until he got to the date that he dropped the clipboard creating a loud thud in the process. He heard a pair of footsteps somewhere in the distance, but his mind was racing.

Two-thousand-forty-two, he thought to himself. *There is no way. Where was I for twenty years?*

Questions flooded his mind faster than he could process them when a nurse ran up to the curtains that separated his bed from the rest of the room. Charlotte moved them aside quickly. "Is everything okay here?"

Kyle shook his head and stood. "Everything is not okay."

Charlotte looked down at the clipboard on the floor. "Kyle, listen to me. I know you have a lot of questions. I promise to get you some answers, but I need you to stay calm."

"Stay calm?" Kyle asked and took a few steps forward. "Why does my chart say that is two-thousand-forty-two?"

Charlotte bit her bottom lip. "Because that's today's date, Kyle."

"Where was I for the last twenty years?" Kyle asked. The panic in his voice became more pronounced with every word. "The last thing I remember is sitting in a locker room in twenty-twenty-two!"

Charlotte took two steps back and looked to her left. "Get Russel in here now!"

Kyle heard a door open and close. "What does Russel have to do with this? Are you holding him here too?"

"We are not holding anyone here," Charlotte said. "Russel is the one that found you. He brought you here."

"None of this makes any sense." Kyle shook his head again. He prepared to run past Charlotte but felt light headed when he jerked his body forward. The room began to spin. He looked at Charlotte, who had her hands up at her sides, motioning for him to settle down. He shook his head, set his sights on the door and brushed past Charlotte.

Kyle didn't know what was happening, but he knew he needed to get some answers.

———

If there was one thing Russel enjoyed on the rare nights that he wasn't on a mission or dealing with some sort of crisis, it was a good night's sleep. He was hoping this would be one of those nights, but when the violent knock on his door came, he knew it wasn't meant to be.

"Russel, get your ass up!" Alex called from out in the hall. "We have a situation."

"Coming out!" Russel got dressed in seconds and swung his door open. "What happened?"

"It's Kyle," Alex said. He led Russel down the hall. A few people cracked the doors open. "Everyone lock your doors! This is not a drill!"

Russel heard locks clicking up and down the hall. "What happened to Kyle?"

"He woke up in a panic," Alex said. "Charlotte tried to speak with him, but he raced out of the room."

"He could barely move an hour ago."

Alex stopped and gave Russel a stern look. "Charlotte says he is moving just fine now. He heals up quickly. It must be a side effect of the stasis, just like your healing ability."

"Wait, you know about that?" Russel was unable to hide the shock on his face.

"I know everything that goes on down here. That's how I keep everyone safe." Alex said. "Now move it. Your friend was last spotted outside of the garage."

———

He had no idea where he was or where he was going, but he knew he needed to get outside. Kyle saw signs that pointed towards a garage and figured it was his best bet. What he did account for was the lack of light in this part of the hall. The only thing he could see was a red Exit sign down the hall, and he walked toward it slowly, trying not to make too much noise.

The light above Kyle turned on, and he instinctively covered his face.

"Kyle, it's Russel. Please stay where you are."

Kyle turned around in time to see Russel running down the hall. He stopped as soon as he spotted Kyle and put his hands up by his shoulders.

"Kyle," Russel said slowly. He was still a few doors away at a safe distance. "Do you remember who I am?"

"Yes," Kyle replied. He looked Russel up and down. "How are you here? And walking? You broke your neck. I saw it. I was right there!"

"Listen! I don't have all of the answers. A lot has happened in the past twenty years. What I can tell you is that you're safe here."

"Twenty years?" Kyle asked and shook his head in disbelief. "You look almost exactly the same as you did that day when…"

"I know Kyle," Russel said with a nod. "You haven't aged either. And there is an explanation for that. Now come with me, and I'll fill you in on as much as I can."

Kyle touched his own face. He didn't feel any different than he did before he woke up. His face should have aged. He looked down at his hands and arms. Everything looked exactly how he remembered it.

Russel approached Kyle slowly and put his arm behind his back. "Everyone that wakes up feels like this."

"I can't believe you're here," Kyle said.

"Well, believe it," Russel said. "You're going to be seeing quite a bit of me."

EIGHT

Terry held the door open for Alex as the two of them walked into the office to join Russel and Kyle.

"Gentlemen," Alex said. He took his seat behind the desk. Terry stood on his left side with his hands behind his back.

"Kyle, this is Alex. He's the man responsible for this underground complex," Russel said. He gestured towards Terry. "This young man here is Terry. He is our best tech guy. He designs all of our gear and encrypts all of our systems to make sure we stay hidden."

Kyle, now dressed in Russel's loose purple T-shirt and a pair of black sweatpants, stood up and shook hands with Alex and Terry. "I apologize for my actions. I'm very confused about what's going on."

"No need to apologize," Alex said. "You're not the first one to cause a scene upon waking up and realizing that you've been in suspended animation for twenty years."

"I'm still coming to grips with that," Kyle rubbed his forehead. "I have a few questions."

"That's part of the reason for this meeting," Alex said.

"What exactly is going on?" Kyle asked. "Why was I asleep for twenty years?"

"Terry, why don't you step in here?" Alex said.

"About twenty years ago, Felix Coleman's company developed a serum that was supposed to be used on violent criminals to stabilize their behavior," Terry began. "Not too long after that Russel suffered his injury. We believe that the accident prompted Felix to go into business with some shady characters. Coleman Tech did not possess the technology needed to save Russel, but one of his business partners did. In exchange for Russel's recovery, Felix shared the formula for the serum with those same business partners, and in the process, the serum was released into Reign's water supply. Felix disappeared shortly after, but the population of this town has been living in constant fear of absolutely everything. Five years after the disappearance of Felix Coleman, the androids appeared to enforce the law, as our existing police force was too afraid to do anything on their own. The law didn't really need enforcing since almost the entire population was exposed to the serum."

"The androids are the things we were running away from?" Kyle asked.

"Yes," Russel replied. "Those were the newest models."

"The androids have an agenda," Terry continued. "That's why we're hiding down here. They kidnap people, especially those that are not affected by the serum. We are not sure what happens to most of them, but we do know that some of them have been turned into androids."

"They also kidnap children," Alex interjected. "We've been trying to put a stop to it for nearly fifteen years, but with most of the population too afraid of their own shadow, it's been an uphill battle."

"That's where we come in," Russel said.

"I tracked down Russel's pod shortly after his father's disappearance," Alex said. "His injury hadn't healed yet, so I had to wait a few years before getting him back out into the world."

"The problem is that there is only so much I can do alone," Russel said. "We need to put a stop to the android's occupation of this city, and to do that, I'm going to need your help."

Kyle crossed his arms and leaned back into his chair. "This is a lot to take in."

"I know," Russel said and his eyes wandered over to Alex.

"As of right now, you, Russel and I are the only ones that haven't been exposed to the serum," Alex said. "We need the two of you to break into their lab and retrieve the original formula. Once we have it, Terry and I can reverse engineer it and create an antidote that we can use to take Reign back."

"Why us?" Kyle asked. "Can't the federal government step in and handle this crisis?"

Terry and Alex exchanged concerned glances. Alex gave a nod of approval, and Terry said; "Reign is cut off from the rest of the world. Coleman Tech sustains every aspect of everyday life in the city. The citizens believe that the outside world is at war and Reign is the only safe place at the moment. There is also a force field around the perimeter of Reign. Nobody can get in or out."

"How is that possible?" Kyle asked.

Terry shrugged. "It shouldn't be possible, but here we are."

"From what little information we've had access to, we know that there were attempts to penetrate the shield from the outside," Kyle said. "It's being monitored by a small group of scientists about twenty miles out. Since it never caused any trouble for the outside world, and it's been more than two decades, it's just kind of been left alone."

"Okay," Kyle said. He was still clearly trying to process everything he had just heard. "None of this explains why I was placed into one of those pods for twenty years. I know Russel was injured, but I was completely fine as far as I can remember."

"The truth is we don't know," Alex said. "I do believe that their lab holds answers to many of our questions. If you and Russel can get in there, we might get some answers for the first time in twenty years."

Kyle nodded with a blank stare. "Wait! If I've been away for twenty years. What happened with my mom and my brother?!"

"I looked for them after Alex found me," Russel said. "There was no sign of them at your old house. I didn't know where else to look."

"We have to go look again!" Kyle said and jumped out of his chair.

Terry glazed over at Alex with a bewildered look on his face. "We don't have the time-"

"We'll have our surveillance team look for them," Alex said and shot a look of disapproval towards Terry. "If we find any clues. You'll be the first to know. In the meantime, we need you to recover from twenty years of stasis."

"I'm completely fine," Kyle protested.

"No, you're not," Alex said. "You've been in stasis for twenty years. We need to know what's going on with you before we send you anywhere."

Kyle was about to argue against more tests when Charlotte burst into the room.

"We have an emergency!" She shouted, clearly out of breath from running. "The Sanford's daughter Lilly was snatched up by an android right outside of the cave!"

"Terry, quick! Head to the surveillance room and see which way they are headed!" Alex ordered. "Russel get-"

"I'm already on it," Russel said and headed for the door.

"I'm coming with you," Kyle said.

"You're not going anywhere," Alex said.

"We can go save the girl or we can stand here and argue, "Kyle said and looked around at everyone in the room.

———

Russel was pulling his suit on with significantly more urgency than ever before. He had seen kids go missing before and the parents were never quite the same after that.

"I'm going with you."

"God, Kyle!" Russel exclaimed and almost fell over as he tried to put on the pants part of his armor. "How did you get here?"

"I followed you," Kyle said. "Listen, I can't stay here."

"Why not?"

"I can't explain it." Kyle looked down at the floor, struggling to find the words. "I lived my whole life in Reign; even if everything changed as much as you say it did, I would still rather be out there. I don't know this place, and I don't know anyone here."

"You know me," Russel said.

"If those things are anything like I remember, you'll need my help."

Russel looked past Kyle and spotted Alex rushing towards them. "Okay, let me talk to him."

Alex walked up to them with his teeth clenched, and his eyes darted from Russel to Kyle. "Listen here, kid. I don't know who you are, but you follow my rules down here!"

Kyle remained silent but did not back away.

With the tension rising, Russel stepped in between them. "Alex, listen, he just emerged from stasis. He only wants to help."

"Then he should do what I say and heal up first," Alex said.

"There is a little girl missing from what I understand," Kyle said. "I want to help get her back. You said it yourself that you want my help."

"When you're ready." Alex insisted.

"The longer we argue, the further the android is going to get with Lilly. We need to go now!" Russel said.

"Fine," Alex said and stepped right up to Kyle. "If anything happens to Russel or the little girl, you'll have to deal with me."

"We'll bring her back," Russel said and pointed to Kyle towards the wall to his right where the spare suits were hanging. "Kyle put one on one of the suits. We are going to have to take the long staircase to avoid giving away our location."

With his gaze still fixed squarely on Kyle, Alex took a few steps back and gave a reluctant nod to the control room.

Terry emerged from behind a row of desks, holding something resembling a large shoebox. "If you're really going out there, you'll need this suit."

Kyle grabbed the box and quickly opened it. "This armor similar to Russel's?"

"Sort of," Terry said, clearly annoyed. "It won't fit as well because I didn't have time to take your measurements."

Kyle began putting on the suit.

"If you survive this mission, I'll see if I can get you a better fitting suit," Terry added. "While we are out there, Russel's code name is Number Two, and yours will be Number Three. Alex is Control."

Kyle struggled with the tight-fitting suit for close to a minute but got it on as quickly as he could.

"This way," Russel said and placed a small earpiece into his right ear. He handed an identical earpiece to Kyle. "The android's last known location is about two miles west."

"Okay," Kyle put in the earpiece and picked up the pace. "How far is the exit?"

As soon as the platform came to a halt, Kyle and Russel took off.

"Number Three," Russel said. "Can you hear me?"

"Yes," Kyle replied through the earpiece.

"The door is right here," Russel said and came to a complete stop. He swung the door open, looked, and led Kyle into a dark cave. "The exit is up ahead. We have to run if we are going to catch this guy."

"Why wouldn't we use the bike you used to get me?" Kyle asked.

"We can't risk attracting the attention of other androids in the area," Russel said and took off.

Kyle's quads and calves tightened up as he took his first stride, but he ignored the pain and kept running.

———

Russel made it to the entrance of the cave first, with Kyle trailing a few feet away. "Not bad for a guy who was in stasis for two decades."

Kyle stopped at the entrance and watched Russel venture into the light outside of the cave. "I'm clearly out of shape."

"No way," Russel said and squinted away from the sun.

"You're out of shape too," Kyle said. "Otherwise, you wouldn't be breathing that heavily."

Russel shook his head and pointed to the right. "Let's go. We have another two miles before we catch up to our target."

As they began to run, Kyle took a quick inventory of his surroundings. He assumed he was in the industrial part of Reign, still a few miles outside of the center of the city. There was a junkyard to his right and a fenced off, rusty warehouse, littered with everything from abandoned cars to loose tires and garbage bags full of random debris.

Russel and Kyle ran at full speed. Once they left the junkyard, there was nothing but perfectly paved two-way road lined with trees. Russel pulled ahead, but Kyle never let himself fall too far behind.

"I think I see them!" Russel said and picked up even more speed.

By the time Kyle caught up to Russel, they hadn't run anywhere close to two miles. Kyle could still see the junkyard behind them, but they were both completely spent nonetheless.

"Are you okay?" Russel asked.

Still breathing heavily, Kyle nodded and looked straight ahead at the android.

"He spotted us," Russel said and stood up straight. "Are you sure you're up for this?"

Kyle stood up straight as well and nodded. They walked side by side and headed towards the android. Lilly was thrown over his shoulder. She was struggling to get free and crying, but it had no effect on her kidnapper. He continued running at a steady pace until he realized that he was being followed. He slowed down and then came to a complete stop without turning around.

"I'm not used to doing this with a partner," Russel admitted. "But we are going to take him together. Our first priority is Lilly's safety, and I'll get the brute's attention. You grab the girl and run her to safety."

"Like you said, we'll take him together," Kyle replied. "I'll make sure the girl is safe."

Russel took off running at the android, who turned around just in time to dodge a flurry of kicks and punches. Kyle came up right behind Russel, and once the android loosened his grip, he quickly snatched the little girl away, prompting her to start crying even louder.

The android shifted his attention to Kyle, who was backpedaling with Lilly in his arms.

Russel jumped on the android's back and wrapped his arms around his neck. "Kyle! Run!"

Kyle picked up the little girl with one arm. He held her tight enough to keep her in place and took off running back towards the junkyard. Kyle turned around once he put about two hundred yards between himself and Russel. He saw that Russel was still going back and forth with the android, clearly trying to buy them some time.

"Lilly, listen to me." Kyle put the girl down on the ground slowly and crouched down. "I'm here to take you back to your parents. I just need you to do something for me."

The little girl stopped crying. Kyle took that as a sign of cooperation.

"I need you to climb down this hill here and hide in the bushes right over there until I come to get you. Can you do that for me?"

Lilly's cheeks were red from crying, but with her lips clenched, she managed to give Kyle a nod.

Kyle watched Lilly walk down the hill very carefully, turning around a few times to make sure he was still there. Once she was all the way down the hill, she looked at the bushes and then back at Kyle.

"Go hide right there." Kyle pointed at the tall bushes

The girl turned around and ran as quickly as she could. Once she was out of sight, Kyle turned back towards Russel and his adversary. The android had the upper hand, and Russel was trying not to get pummeled.

Kyle sprinted towards Russel. His heart felt like it was beating out of his chest. He decided to focus on the task at hand and analyzed his target. The android was at least half a foot taller than Kyle with legs as thick as tree trunks and massive back. He had what Kyle assumed was the standard android gear; a black armor that closely resembled riot gear, combat boots, and a pair of reflective goggles that covered everything above the nose.

He wasn't exactly in peak physical condition, but Kyle believed that if he picked up enough speed, his momentum would be enough to knock that mountain of a man off his feet. He braced for impact and hit the android with everything he had only to witness himself bouncing off the bigger man and falling flat on his back.

As Kyle laid there in disbelief, it quickly became apparent that he was able to least draw the enemy's attention. He felt the ground tremble, and he rolled out of the way just as one of the combat boots had landed exactly where his face would have been.

Kyle got back on his feet and took a few deep breaths as the android stalked him. He took a quick glance at Russel who was still down but was making progress toward regaining a vertical base.

"Kyle, we've got to go," Russel muttered.

With his breathing under control, Kyle stopped and put his hands up, ready to defend himself. "I need to see what this brute is made of."

Russel realized that Kyle wasn't listening and charged at the android from behind as soon as he made it to his feet. The sneak attack backfired as the android grabbed Russel with both hands and threw him against the closest tree.

"Russel, no!" Kyle shouted as he watched his friend hit the tree and land on his side with a thud

Russel's failed attack created an opening that Kyle desperately needed. It didn't take long for that to register. While the android was still focused on Russel, Kyle ran up, grabbed his right leg, and used his own legs to sweep the much bigger man off his feet. The android was able to grab on to Kyle, sending both of them crashing to the ground.

Kyle was fully aware that if he wanted to come out of this encounter alive, he'd have to keep the android under him at all times. He delivered a few quick elbow strikes directly at the android's face, forcing him to defend himself.

"Kyle," Russel said, using his arm to pick himself up off the ground. "You need to get the girl and run!"

"Not a chance!" Kyle replied, still wrestling for control. He managed to knock off the android's goggles, sending him into a temporary retreat.

Kyle stepped forward in pursuit when the android put one hand in front of him and grabbed his head with the other one.

"Kyle?" The android asked. Both of his hands were holding his head, and he fell down to his knees.

"How do you know my name?" Kyle asked. He took a few steps towards Russel in case this was some kind of trick.

"Is that really you?"

Russel pulled himself up off the ground and limped towards Kyle.

"I don't know how this is even possible," the android said. His eyes remained fixed on Kyle.

"Has one of them ever recognized you before?" Kyle asked quietly.

"I've never even heard them speak," Russel replied.

"It's me, Kyle. It's Timmy."

Kyle's heart began to beat so hard he couldn't hear anything else around him. He took a closer look at the android that had collapsed in front of him. He resembled his brother in many ways. Same hair color, similar nose, but most importantly, he had his brother's blue eyes. It had been twenty years since Kyle went missing. His five-year-old brother would be about the same age as the android in front of him.

"This is some kind of android trick, Kyle," Russel said.

"It's no trick," the android shook his head and grabbed it with both hands.

"If it's really you Timmy," Kyle said and took a few steps forward. "How did you end up like this?"

"We have to go, Kyle. We don't have time for this." Russel looked around nervously.

"Your friend is right," Timmy said. "When I disobeyed the order to take you down, reinforcements were dispatched right away. There are four advanced units six minutes away."

Kyle turned back towards Russel. "Grab Lilly, and I'll meet you by the gate in a minute."

Russel nodded reluctantly and limped off.

"Tell me one thing," Kyle said. "Where is Mom? Is she…"?

"I can't remember the last time I saw her," Timmy said. "Time is all jumbled up in my head. You need to find her. We had a rendezvous point in case we got separated. I can't remember exactly where, but Mom had it written down on the yellow pad, and she always kept it next to the phone."

"Come with us," Kyle said. "The people I'm with can help you."

"I can't do that Kyle," Timmy said and began to stand up. "You need to run as fast as you can. I'm being reprogrammed as we speak. In three minutes, I'll attack you along with four others."

Kyle began to back pedal and looked back towards Russel, who motioned for him to hurry.

"I'm going to find mom," Kyle said. "And then I'm coming to get you. No number of androids are going to stand in my way."

"Don't tell mom you found me like this, and don't come after me," Timmy said. "Now run and don't look back!"

Kyle saw a blank expression take over his brother's face. He was running out of time. As much as it pained him, he turned around and sprinted towards Russel.

"What did he say to you?" Russel asked. He was holding Lilly in his arms.

"He told me where to find my mom."

"You can't trust him. He is under their control."

"He could have killed us both if he wanted to," Kyle said.

"We have to go. There is no way we can take on five of those things."

Kyle looked back at Timmy. His facial expression remained blank.

"Number Two! Were you able to get Lilly?" Alex's voice fed into the ear pieces with some static.

Russel put his index finger on the ear piece. "We did. We are on the way back now."

"We have a situation," Alex said. "There are two androids about thirty seconds away."

"That's too close," Russel said. "We would lead them right to the base."

"You need to find a place to hide," Alex suggested.

"It sounds like this whole place will be crawling with androids soon," Kyle said. "I'll lead them away. You take the girl back."

"What? No!" Russel shook his head as Lilly began to sob. "You saw what one of them can do; there is no way you can outrun two of them."

"I'll figure something out," Kyle said. "Control, how far are they?"

"You got fifteen seconds to find a hiding spot," Alex replied.

"I think that shed over there is our best bet," Kyle said.

Russel clenched his teeth and looked at the shed and then back at Kyle. "Fine. Keep your earpiece on. As soon as it's safe, I'll get in touch and guide you back to the base."

Kyle nodded.

"Get to that shed!" Alex said.

Russel sprinted to the shed, swung the door open, and closed it softly.

Kyle looked around and spotted the two androids a few yards

away. He started walking towards them until he was sure that they could see him.

"Number Three, they've spotted you," Alex said. "Run."

The Androids began their approach towards Kyle. His heart was beating almost as fast as it was during the fight. He looked at the two androids and took off, running back towards the road.

"Don't look back," Alex instructed. "Just keep moving."

Kyle looked back and saw that the androids were gaining on him.

"They don't get tired, and they don't slow down," Alex said. "You better find a place to hide quickly."

Kyle picked up the pace while controlling his breathing. He spotted some townhouses a few yards ahead and figured that would be the best place to lose the androids.

He looked back once again before entering what looked like an abandoned neighborhood on the outskirts of Reign. He ran through the streets full of overgrown lawns and rusty fences. He needed a place he could slip into without having to make much noise. As bad as the houses looked, he had yet to see one with an open door or a broken window.

Kyle heard the footsteps of his pursuers as he turned the corner and ran past a few shops.

Not a single broken window? Really? He thought to himself as the effects of fatigue began to set into his lungs and quads. *I need to find a place quickly.*

The noise of the androids on his tail was drowned out by another sound. This one was much less menacing but also felt out of place.

Either that's an Ice Cream truck, or I'm seriously losing my mind, Kyle thought to himself but instinctively followed the sound. *If it got my attention, it probably got their attention too.*

Kyle slowed down at the intersection but didn't see the ice cream truck. He sprinted to the next street and spotted the vehicle moving at a leisurely speed, as most ice cream trucks do. He turned, ran towards the music, and tried to catch a glimpse of who was driving. All he could see were two hairy hands gripping the steering wheel. He didn't have the time for a closer look and committed to running right past the truck when another set of hands reached out of the passenger side door and pulled him right inside.

A man dressed in the traditional white ice cream parlor uniform slammed Kyle against the wall and put his index finger over his nose and mouth.

Kyle could barely breath, and talking was definitely out of the question. He examined the crew of the ice cream truck to see if they were androids, and quickly became apparent that they weren't. The man holding Kyle against the wall was a few inches shorter than him; he had thinning hair with a five o'clock shadow that started right under his eyes and went all the way down his neck. The driver was a stocky man with short white hair that matched the uniform that was clearly a size too small. His stomach remained pressed up against the steering wheel when he turned around and gave his partner a nod.

"We're in the clear," said the man who was holding Kyle and let him go with caution. "You're not heavy enough to be an Android, and you're not in a complete panic, so who are you?"

"You two snatched me off the street," Kyle said. "Why don't you tell me who you are first? Then tell me what that was all about."

"Ungrateful little prick, isn't he?" The driver mumbled without taking his eyes off the road.

The man who snatched Kyle put his hands up by his chest and forced a smile. "My name is Wayne, and the grump at the wheel is my business partner, Marshall. Now we know you're not one of those freaky robots running around this town, but we need to know who you are."

"I'm Kyle. You're correct in your assessment. I'm not an android."

"Okay. Let's have a seat," Wayne said and pointed to a pair of coolers in the middle of the truck.

"Look, I'm kind of in a rush-"

"If you step outside of this truck, those things will snatch you up," Marshall said from the front.

"He is not exaggerating, you know," Wayne said and sat down on the cooler.

Kyle sat down across from him slowly.

"Tell me. Are you from the outside?" Wayne asked.

"If you mean outside of this town, then no," Kyle said.

"So how come you're not paralyzed by fear like everyone else here?"

"I'm not sure," Kyle said. "I was in some sort of stasis for the past 20 years. I woke up to this world only a few hours ago."

"Stasis," Wayne said as if trying to analyze the word's meaning. "If this was three months ago, I would have called you crazy, but Marshall and I have seen things in this town that I've only seen in movies."

"You mean the androids?" Kyle asked.

Marshall and Wayne exchanged glances and shook their heads.

"Are you convinced that he is telling the truth?" Wayne asked. "Because I am."

Marshall nodded without taking eyes off the road.

"What are you guys doing here?" Kyle said and looked around the inside of the worn-out truck. There were bags of clothes piled up in the back, along with a variety of canned foods. The walls were lined with ice cream dispensers, cones, cups, and lids. "You're clearly not selling a ton of ice cream."

Wayne looked back at Marshall, who shrugged first and then gave a soft nod of approval.

"We bought this truck last year and have been looking for a place to set up a nice little route," Wayne said. "All the towns for the next hundred miles had ice cream trucks, except for Reign. We came here to do a trial run for six weeks. That was three months ago, and have been stuck here ever since."

"What's preventing you from leaving? The androids?" Kyle asked.

"Yes and no," Wayne replied. "The androids are a problem, but they don't go inside the truck for some strange reason. What's even more unusual is that once we turn on the truck music, they completely disregard us. The real problem is the damn force field around this whole town. We've been driving all over the outskirts of this town trying to find an opening, but as you can see, we are still here."

Kyle took a moment to process what Wayne told him. His initial thought was to tell Wayne and Marshall about the underground base. Even though they seemed genuine and shared some information with him, Kyle still wasn't sure if he could trust them with information that might endanger everyone at the base.

"Have you looked for others like yourselves?" Kyle asked cautiously. "I'm sure you're not the only ones trying to find a way out."

"There are others," Wayne said with little enthusiasm. "But they are trying to take down the whole android operation here. We are not trying to join some kind of rebel group. We just want to get out of this town and get home to our families."

Kyle assumed the others Wayne was referring to were the people living at the base but he pretended like the information was new to him.

"So, what's your plan, kid?" Marshall asked.

"I'm trying to make it back to my house on the other side of town," Kyle said. "I'm looking for my mom."

"The last time you saw her was before your stasis?" Wayne asked.

"Yes."

"Your Mom is probably a zombie, just like everyone else in this town," Marshall said.

"Marshall, come on!" Wayne said. "Don't be such a prick."

Marshall disregarded Wayne and kept driving.

"Have you had any contact with her?' Wayne asked.

"No," Kyle admitted. "I just need to get to the house. Once I'm sure my mom is safe, I'll probably be looking to get out of here just like you two."

"Okay," Wayne said. He clasped his hands together and stood up. "Marshall, I'll take the wheel now."

Marshall checked the rearview mirrors and pulled over. He stood up, and Wayne took his place. Kyle underestimated how big Marshall was while he was behind the wheel. He was too tall to stand up straight in the truck and had to crouch down to walk over to the cooler where Wayne was sitting.

Once Marshall sat down, Wayne shifted into the drive and pulled away from the curb.

"I see Alex is getting very creative in his recruitment methods," Marshall said and brushed his thick mustache with one hand.

"What?" Kyle asked with a straight face.

"Your story was cute," Marshall said and leaned forward. "But we've been around here long enough to know that the armor you're wearing comes from that secret base somewhere in this part of town."

Kyle took a deep breath but remained silent.

"The answer is still no," Marshall continued. "We have no interest in getting caught up in any conflicts in this weird town. Especially if it involves tussling with those walking tin cans out there."

"Let me get this straight," Kyle said. "You think that someone sent me out here to risk my life running from those things, just so that I can run into you two? "

"Desperate times call for desperate measures," Marshall said.

"Okay," Kyle said and stood up. "I'm only out here to find my mom. I don't care about any underground bases and definitely don't care about recruiting two guys in an ice cream truck to fight some robots."

"I told you he wasn't here to recruit us," Wayne called from the front.

"Shut it, Wayne!" Marshall yelled back. He stood up and looked down on Kyle, who didn't budge, before walking back towards the driver's seat.

Kyle watched the two men have a quiet discussion but couldn't quite make out what was being said. Wayne let Marshall climb back into the driver seat while making his way back towards Kyle.

"Let's all just take it easy," Wayne said with a reassuring smile. He sat back down on the cooler and motioned for Kyle to do the same.

Kyle looked over towards Marshall and then around the ice cream truck to make sure this wasn't some kind of trap. He reluctantly sat back down.

"We don't want any trouble," Wayne said. "Marshall has a newborn at home. I have a wife and two kids. The one thing we all have in common is that we are all trying to get home. How about we give you a ride to your house, and we all go our separate ways?"

"Works for me," Kyle said.

"Very well then," Wayne said. "What's the address?"

"Just head straight for about four miles on this road," Kyle said. "I'll let you know where to make the turn."

"You heard that, Marshall?"

Marshall gave Wayne a look through the rearview mirror and kept driving.

"I don't know if you heard that grunt, but that means Marshall is on board with dropping you off," Wayne said.

"Thanks," Kyle said. Loud enough for both men to hear him.

"You want ice cream?" Wayne asked. "We ran out of sprinkles last week, but we are still good on pretty much everything else."

"What? You're actually selling ice cream here?"

"We have to survive somehow," Wayne said with a shrug. "Vanilla or chocolate? The first cone is on me."

———

Lilly squeezed Russel's hand as the two of them descended towards a crowd of two dozen people in the control room. With the adrenaline wearing off, Russel could feel a pounding headache coming on. His ribs were sore and it took all that was left of his strength to remain standing.

As the platform came to a halt, Lily's parents rushed forward, and the girl ran into their arms for an embrace they thought might never happen. The father was the first to let go and walked over to Russel who was gingerly walking down the five steps from the platform down onto the main floor.

"Russel," the father extended his right hand. "We are forever in your debt."

"Your little girl was very brave out there, Brandon," Russel said and shook his hand.

"You need help getting to the medical wing?"

"I'll be fine. Go be with your family."

Alex and Terry entered through the double doors on the opposite side of the room and made their way through the crowd until they reached Russel.

Terry ran in front of Alex soon as he got close enough to see the shape that Russel was in. "Russel, you need to go see Charlotte right away!"

"I'm okay," Russel lied and almost collapsed, but Terry caught him and put Russel's arm around his neck.

"Obviously not," Terry said just as Alex approached them after making a brief stop to speak with Lily and her parents.

"Everyone, please make your way back up to the main floor," Alex said to the crowd behind them before shifting his attention to Russel. "You look like crap."

"Thanks boss," Russel said and attempted to crack a smile. "We have a problem."

"I'm well aware," Alex said and looked Russel up and down. "You need to let Charlotte examine you."

"We need to go after Kyle," Russel said and instantly regretted taking a deep breath as he felt a sharp pain in his ribs.

"You need to rest," Alex said. "Terry and I are monitoring Kyle's location through the tracker in his suit. I'm assuming he is going back to his childhood home. As soon as the number of androids on the streets drops down, we'll go out there and get him."

"You can't go out there alone," Russel said. "Come and get me as soon as you ready."

"Terry, take him to see Charlotte," Alex ordered, ignoring Russel's request. "Then meet me in my office. Russel, you have the rest of the night off."

Terry nodded and helped Russel towards the exit.

Alex stood at the foot of the stairs and enjoyed a rare moment of silence. He pulled a small tablet out of his pocket and looked at the blinking blue light, which showed Kyle's location. While Russel spoke very highly of him, Alex did not expect the young man to take on one android and somehow outrun four more in broad daylight when the streets were swarming with them. Alex watched the blinking get slower until it became a solid blue dot. He put the tablet back in his pocket and headed back to his office to prepare for his first trip to the surface in six months.

———

The underground complex was connected by more hallways and staircases than Russel cared to count, but after two years of living there, he knew exactly where everything was. He could find the Medical Bay with his eyes closed, and he was fairly certain that he was its most frequent visitor.

He hobbled in still leaning on Terry, and was surprised to find Charlotte behind her desk at the far end of the room. She was looking over her notes but looked up as soon as Terry and Russel appeared in the doorway.

"Russel! My God!" she exclaimed and launched herself out of her chair.

"He is all yours," Terry said.

"Let's put him right here," Charlotte ran over to the curtain that separated the first bed from the rest of the office and pulled it back.

"Thanks, Terry. I got it from here." Russel knew the procedure. He limped over to the examination table and grimaced as he sat down.

"I've seen you look a lot worse." She looked him up and down as he removed his armor.

Once he was down to his sleeveless undershirt and shorts, Charlotte began her examination by checking his eyes and the bruises around his face.

"You want to tell me about the mission?" Charlotte asked while shining a light into Russel's eyes.

"The mission was a success," Russel said as he followed the light. "I can't help but think how many of these kidnappings we could have stopped if Kyle was around earlier. He distracted those androids, so he is still out there. I hope he is okay."

Charlotte switched the light off. "You did your best, Russel. No one blames you for those kidnappings."

Russel sighed and looked away. "Thirteen children went missing without a trace, Charlotte. I still see their parents in the halls. They are never going to recover from what happened."

"Look at me, Russel." Charlotte gently cupped his chin with her gloved hand. "You were just a kid when Alex found you in that pod. You weren't trained for any of this. None of us really were. You and

Alex are the only ones who were not exposed to the toxin. And you're the only one that's still capable of going up to the surface."

"Now, it's not just me. We've got Kyle," Russel said optimistically.

"Speaking of Kyle," Charlotte walked back towards her desk and grabbed a clipboard. "The blood work results from his initial exam are here. It looks like he has traces of the toxin in his blood, but it's nothing like the people we brought in from the surface. A very tiny amount, and it's pretty much out of his system."

"It's hard for me to believe he had any toxin in him at all," Russel said. "He went toe to toe with an android out there. Anyone exposed to the toxin would run at the thought of a one-on-one confrontation with any of those things."

———

The ice cream truck's brakes let out a low squeal as it came to a halt outside of Kyle's house. Wayne slid the door open and hopped out. Kyle followed him out while Marshall remained behind the wheel.

"I don't think anyone is home" Wayne whispered and pointed at dark windows.

"I still need to go inside" Kyle said and turned to walk towards the front door. "I hope you guys find a way out of here soon."

"Wait," Wayne said and reached out for a handshake.

Kyle looked down and saw folded up paper in Wayne's hand. He raised his eyebrows and waited for an explanation.

Wayne looked back at Marshall, who had dosed off with his head titled back. "Take this. It has my number on it. If you find a way out, reach out to us."

"Okay," Kyle said and took the paper.

"And if you're ever in a pinch," Wayne looked back to make sure Marshall was still sleeping. "Give me a call, and if I can help, I will."

"I thought you didn't want to get involved," Kyle said.

"We don't," Wayne said. "But if I have to get us involved in something that leads us out of here, I might be able to get Marshall to reconsider."

"I see," Kyle nodded. "Thanks again for the rescue."

"Take care of yourself," Wayne said and jogged back to the truck.

Kyle examined the outside of the house and knew that the chances of his mom waiting for him inside were slim at best. The grass that he used to trim every other week was completely overgrown. The windows were so dusty that it was visible from a distance. His mom would never allow that. To make things worse, when Kyle got close to the door, the knob was completely covered in rust. He tried to open the door, but it was locked.

There were three flower pots on each side of the patio, and Kyle remembered that there was always an emergency set of keys under one of them.

If I remember correctly, Kyle thought as he approached the middle pot on the left side and lifted it, *there it is.*

He reached down and grabbed two silver keys, which should have been taped to the bottom of the pot, but just like Kyle's hopes of seeing his mom at the house, the tape had almost completely disintegrated.

Kyle was able to open the door on the first try and entered a dark and damp living room. "Anyone here?"

When there was no answer, Kyle used what little daylight was left to walk through the first floor of the house. He found a picture frame in the living room with Timmy, their mom, and him at Six Flags. It was from the summer before his junior year of High School.

Has it really been over twenty years?

Kyle opened the latches on the back of the frame and took the picture out. He placed it in his pocket and decided to avoid the second floor. He knew there was nothing but more memories there, and he didn't have time to sit and reminisce. Kyle went into the kitchen and headed straight for the clipboard that his mom used to leave notes and appointment cards. He ripped off the appointment cards one by one until he spotted a handwritten note with *14 Treemont Ave* written in bright red. Kyle flipped the note over in search of additional clues and found a small sticker on the back that read *Lost and Found.*

Kyle shuffled through the rest of the papers on the clipboard but didn't find anything more useful than that note. He shoved into his pocket with the picture and took one last look around the kitchen where so many meals, laughs, and even a few arguments took place.

As Kyle tried to push the memories to the back of his mind, he heard static in his ear, followed by a somewhat familiar voice.

"Number Three," Alex said. "Are you there?"

"I'm here."

"Find what you were looking for?"

"Sort of."

"I need you to head two blocks to the left. There is a construction zone that leads into the sewers. Head down there quickly; we don't have much time."

"The sewer? Really? I'd rather fight another android."

"You have three minutes," Alex replied, unamused.

NINE

"We're here," Alex said. "This is as close as we can get to the base through the sewer system. Help me lift up the cover from your end."

Kyle was laying in what he could only describe as jet powered sled with a cover. Alex was almost completely horizontal in the front, steering with two joysticks at his sides. Kyle laid in the back behind him with a view of the top of the sewer system.

They lifted the lid together, and Kyle hopped out while Alex struggled to get himself out. Kyle extended his arm out for assistance, and Alex grabbed it reluctantly.

"You're hurt?" Kyle asked as he watched Alex step into the sewer water that reached both of their ankles.

"I'm recovering from a minor knee surgery," Alex said. He pointed to a dim light a few feet away. "That's the exit."

Even though Kyle was ready to leave the sewer as fast as possible, he let Alex lead the way. When they reached the ladder, Alex motioned for Kyle to climb out first. He heard no objections from the young man.

Kyle pulled himself up and watched Alex climb out slowly.

They made their way to the platform. Alex clicked on his earpiece and said, "We're in position."

The platform started moving down slowly. There were small bulbs on the outside of the platform, producing just enough light for Kyle to see Alex's armor. It was burgundy, and the fit wasn't as tight as Kyle's or Russel's. There was a lot more padding around the knees, especially the right knee which explained why Alex put more weight on the left one.

"I'm only going to say this once," Alex said over the hissing of the platform. "You don't run off like that again on your own. You put yourself and everyone down here in danger."

"Someone had to lead the androids away from Russel and the little girl," Kyle objected.

"You didn't have to go all the way to the other side of town," Alex said. "There are plenty of hiding places in the industrial area."

"I had a lead, and I had to follow it."

"You think you're the only one with missing family members?" Alex raised his voice. "We operate as a team down here. If you run off again, no one is coming after you."

The platform slowed down and revealed a nearly empty control room. There were three people spread out at different terminals. The slender young woman with identical red braids hanging down on her shoulders stood up and said, "Welcome back, sir."

"Karen, do me a favor and check if Charlotte has an opening in medical," Alex said.

The girl punched some keys and said, "She has someone in there now. The next opening is in forty-five minutes."

Alex looked over at Kyle and took a deep breath.

"It gives you some time to show him around if you're up for it," Karen added. "Or I can do it. It's up to you."

"You are going to be trouble on the surface and down here," Alex mumbled before turning to Karen. "I'll give him the tour. You can show him where the kids hang out another time. If he sticks around."

Karen started to blush and quickly dropped back into her chair and hid behind her monitor.

"Follow me," Alex said and led Kyle out of the room through a pair of sliding doors.

"I know things have been happening very quickly since your

arrival. It can't be easy waking up from a twenty-year slumber into a not so brave new world."

"We can finally agree on something."

The two of them made their way down a dimply lit hallway just wide enough for two people to walk shoulder to shoulder. Another pair of sliding doors hissed open, and Alex motioned for Kyle to go first. They walked down the hall in relative silence, with Alex occasionally greeting someone in the hall.

"Where are we going exactly?" Kyle asked.

"To the lounge," Alex replied enthusiastically. "Ever since you arrived, it's been nothing but meetings and the control room. I want you to see that this place is so much more than that."

"Is Russel alright?"

"He's a little beat up, but he's been through worse."

They walked for a few more minutes before arriving at a well-lit and furnished room full of small round tables and chairs. There was a traditional bar along the wall to the right and an old-fashioned piano on the opposite side. There were a few people occupying the area with only a single attendant at the bar.

"Have a seat with me right over there by the windows," Alex said and led Kyle towards the floor to ceiling windows directly ahead of them.

Kyle was about to take a seat when he looked out of the windows into what could only be described as farmland a few stories down below. Large sun lamps were hanging off the ceiling, illuminating countless crops and workers as far as the eye could see. There was also modern farm equipment, everything from sprinklers to tractors.

"This is amazing," Kyle said. He sat down without taking his eyes off everything that was going on down below. "You've got a whole farm underground."

"The farm is just a fraction of what goes on down here," Alex said proudly. "We are a fully functioning community down here. Safe from the disaster that's been taking place up above ground."

"How did this all come together?" Kyle asked.

"This was a passion project of mine back when I used to work for Coleman Tech," Alex began. "When things started going south up above, I made sure this project was completed and its exact location remained hidden from the general public. The only way people make it down is if someone on my team finds them and brings them in."

"Look, this is all very impressive," Kyle admitted. "But what's happening on the surface is not okay. You've got robotically enhanced beings kidnapping children while everyone else lives in some kind of warped reality where they're afraid of their own shadow."

"Believe me, I'm well aware of what's going on up there," Alex said. "It's a wicked experiment being run on a town full of innocent people. I'm doing everything in my power to put an end to it, but it's a little tough when almost everyone down here is too afraid to go outside. Never mind taking the fight to one of the androids you and Russel faced earlier."

"Well, we need to put a stop to it and soon," Kyle said. "I saw my brother, who was somehow retrofitted into a nearly unstoppable fighting machine. We need to track down whoever is responsible and fix what's going on up there."

"Your brother?" Alex asked and leaned back in his chair. "Are you sure?"

"Honestly, I'm not one hundred percent sure," Kyle said. "I was hoping you or someone on your team could help me out with that."

"The android spoke to you?"

"Briefly. He's the one that gave me the clue about where to find my mom. Then he said he was being reprogrammed and told me to run."

"I'm not saying that I don't believe you," Alex said and scratched his chin. "But we need to tread lightly. This could be an elaborate scheme to lure us into a trap."

Kyle nodded in agreement. "I think we need to confirm if that was indeed my brother."

"Okay, we'll start there," Alex said. He clicked a button on his watch. "Terry, Kyle, and I are coming down to the lab. Pull up the profiles of all of the known androids."

"You mean to tell me you have a database on all of the androids?" Kyle asked.

"We've got a lot more than that down in the lab kid," Alex said and stood up. "Let's go, we've got work to do."

———

Terry's lab was the exact opposite of what Kyle thought it would be. In his mind, labs had to be well lit areas with plenty of computers and a relatively large number of people working together.

What awaited Kyle inside the lab was a room with minimal lighting and one large monitor in the center of the room, with Terry sitting behind it.

"I have the list pulled up here," Terry said.

Alex headed straight over to Terry's terminal, while Kyle took in his surroundings. There were charts and maps of different places all around Reign. There were headshots of different androids and their last known locations. There were also diagrams of the anatomies of the different android models. Kyle made his way towards Terry's desk slowly while looking at the different headshots in an attempt to match one with the android that claimed to be his brother.

"You're not going to find him over there," Terry said as if he had read Kyle's mind. "He is one of the new models. I don't have much information on him yet, but whatever I do have will be in this database."

Alex motioned for Kyle to come around the desk to join him behind Terry's monitor, which he did.

"This database holds the DNA of every person living in Reign. I ran the DNA that Charlotte was able to extract off of Russel's armor, and I believe we have a match," Terry said.

He proceeded to punch a few keys on his keyboard, and a blurry headshot popped on the screen. "Give it a second."

A few seconds later, the picture came into focus, along with a name.

"Timothy Trevor," Kyle could not believe the words that he'd just read off the screen. "It's really him."

"Indeed," Alex said. "However, that should not earn him your trust. He is still programmed by the enemy."

"Alex is right," Terry said. "He is one of the newer models, which means he was probably integrated less than a year ago. It's hard to believe that he was able to defy his programming. It should be almost impossible."

"He didn't defy it for long," Kyle admitted. "Just long enough to give us a chance to escape."

"Or he was allowed to defy his programming just long enough to give you the location of where they'll be expecting you to show up next." Terry countered.

"And this time it won't be just one unit waiting for you," Terry added. "There will be more of them than you can handle. You barely escaped one of them."

"So, I'm supposed to just forget about my mother?" Kyle asked.

"Of course not," Alex said. "But you do need to give us time to come up with a plan."

"Well, how long do you need?" Kyle asked impatiently.

"Terry, I need you to give me everything you know about that location," Alex said. "We'll send a drone out there, see if we can spot your mother, and then go from there."

"Alright," Kyle replied, trying his best to mask his dissatisfaction.

"In the meantime, I need you to report to the Medical Bay," Alex said. "Charlotte needs to make sure you're cleared to return to the surface."

"I feel fine," Kyle said.

"Listen, kid." Alex gave him a stern look. "We have rules here. Everyone that comes back from a mission, especially one that involves contact with an android, is required to go through a medical exam."

"I'll head there now," Kyle said. "Thanks for your help."

Alex and Terry waited for Kyle to exit the room.

"He is not the easiest person to deal with," Terry spoke up.

"It can't be easy waking up from a twenty-year sleep and coming face to face with an altered version of your little brother," Alex said. "We'll cut him some slack."

"I'm close to decrypting the exact location of the Android base," Terry said. "Once I have it, we are going to have to plan the mission quickly."

"Do you think they know that we've retrieved the file?"

"If they don't know already, there is a good possibility they will know once I break the encryption," Terry said.

"Russel is going to have his hands full on this mission," Alex said.

"Kyle has other things on his mind, but I think he'll come through for us. If you're up for it, I'd like you to go along with them on this mission."

Terry pushed his computer chair away from his desk and placed his hands on his quads. "I want to go. I just don't know if I'll be able to hold it together out in the field."

"I believe in you kid," Alex said and placed his hand on Terry's shoulder. "I always have, and I always will."

"The toxin hasn't been spotted in my system for nearly a year," Terry said. "But I still freeze up when those things get close to me."

"It's okay to be afraid. Everyone is scared of those things, even people like Russel and myself who were never exposed to the toxin."

"I'll make my decision once we have the location," Terry said. "I just don't want to sabotage the mission."

"I wouldn't ask you to go if this wasn't the most important mission we'll probably ever go on," Alex admitted. "But if we can infiltrate their base, we can really turn this thing around."

————

10 Years Ago...

The construction of the underground farm complex was nearly complete. Alex had managed to keep the location a secret during its five-year process. It wasn't as difficult as he had initially anticipated. With Felix focused solely on the production of the android units, everything else was put on the back burner. Even his visits down to the secret lab that contained the floating body of his son became less and less frequent.

Alex was at the point where he was looking to fill key positions down in the complex. He had personally prescreened every candidate and took every precaution possible. He knew that if he made one wrong contact, his entire operation might be put at risk. Time was running out, and he still had a very important positions to fill; the head of security.

It was a breezy autumn night when Alex arrived at the front door of his number one candidate for that position. Howard Lane was a retired police officer with an outstanding record. He was a consultant for Coleman Tech, but he wasn't as plugged in as a lot of the other security workers. Alex believed he was the perfect man for the job.

He rang the doorbell and waited patiently. He heard commotion on the other side of the door and gave it a few minutes before he rang the doorbell once more.

This time the door inched open, and Howard's sweaty, square head, with a mustache and slicked-back hair, peered out. "Alex? What can I do for you?"

"Howard, I was hoping to speak with you about something rather important," Alex said. "Can I come in?"

"Right now is not a good time," Howard said. "We are actually getting ready to leave town."

"To go where exactly?" Alex asked. "You know Reign has been placed in quarantine, right?"

"Something fishy is going on here Alex, and you know it."

"That's why I'm here. I need your help."

"I'll let you in because you've always been straight with me," Howard said. He swung the door open. "But I'm going to have to pat you down first."

Alex raised his eyebrows in surprise, but ultimately complied.

Howard patted him down and let him in.

Alex walked down the hall and into a living room with bare walls. There was only a couch in the center of the room pointed towards a wall where a TV used to hang. There were half a dozen black suitcases on the right side of the couch, along with a few hangers of suit jackets on top of them.

"You were serious about leaving," Alex said as he looked around.

A little boy no older than eight popped his head out of the next room.

"Come on out Terrance," Howard said. "Say hello to Alex."

The little boy had straight black hair with bangs down to his eyebrows. He was wearing sweatpants and a loose T-shirt. He emerged from the room, walked straight up to Alex, and reached up to shake his hand. "I'm Terrance. Nice to meet you."

"Hello, Terrance," Alex shook his hand.

"Go finish packing Terry," Howard said, and the boy disappeared back into his room. "Let's have a seat in the dining room."

Howard led the way, and Alex followed him into a spacious dining room with a round wooden table, four padded chairs, and a large clock on the wall.

Alex took a seat. "Howard, I'm going to get straight to the point."

"Please do."

"I know that you've noticed odd things taking place at Coleman Tech, and all over town," Alex began. "Coleman Tech is responsible for all of it; the kidnapping, the quarantine, the paranoia."

"Why are you telling me this now?" Howard asked.

"Because I know you're looking for a way out," Alex said and leaned in. "And I can offer you the closest thing to that."

"The closest thing to a way out?"

"Yes." Alex reached into his pocket and retrieved his tablet. He pushed a few buttons and slid it across the table.

Howard examined each image before scrolling over to the next one. "You expect me to believe this place is real?"

"It's very real," Alex said. "I've been working on it in secret for nearly five years. It was simply a passion project before I saw where things were going here in Reign. It's a fully equipped underground shelter. There is a farm system for a sustainable food supply, living quarters for two hundred people, and a security system that will keep everyone safe until this quarantine is lifted."

Howard tapped his index finger on the table before looking up at Alex. "What do you need from me?"

"I want you to be head of security," Alex replied. "In return, you and your son will have refuge down there for as long as this lasts."

"The higher-ups at Coleman Tech don't know about this location?"

"I've taken every precaution to ensure they don't find out."

"And none of the androids are going to be down there?"

"None at all. Those things are way too dangerous and unpredictable."

Howard continued to look down at the table and tapped his index finger until he looked up and reached across the table with his right hand. "You have a deal. But only on one condition."

"Name it."

"We leave tonight."

"We can leave right now."

Howard nodded in agreement, and the two men stood up from their seats. They made it back into the living room just as three round black objects crashed through the windows and landed right at their feet with a hissing sound.

"Grenade!" Howard yelled. He grabbed Alex by his jacket and shoved him towards his son's room. "Get down!"

A loud blast went off, shattering every glass window and sending Alex flying into Terry's room.

"Daddy!" Terry screamed and ran towards the door.

Alex regained his balance in time to catch the kid before he could get close to the flames. He crouched down and looked the boy right in the face. "Terry, listen to me. You need to stay right here. I'm going to get your dad, okay?"

The boy nodded with tears streaming down his face.

With the temperature steadily increasing, Alex shed his jacket before making his way toward the fire. He used his hands to protect his mouth from all of the smoke as he jumped over the smaller fires on the living room floor. He saw Howard in a seated position against the wall with flames creeping up to him.

"Howard!" Alex shouted as loud as he could over the crackling of the fire. "I'm coming for you!"

With blood streaming down his face, Howard looked over in Alex's direction and used the wall for support to try to stand up.

"I'm here, Howard," Alex said. He threw the injured man's arm over his shoulder and attempted to help him move towards Terry's room.

"Stop." Howard removed his arm from Alex's shoulder. "There is a trap door under Terry's bed. Use it to get yourself and my son to safety."

"What about you?" Alex asked, even though he saw where the conversation was headed.

"You and I both know what's happening here," Howard said. "They are going to come here and make sure the job is finished."

Alex nodded. He had seen the encrypted files for android routes in the Coleman Tech systems. Now he knew why they were encrypted.

"Keep my son close," Howard said. The sound of heavy footsteps drew his attention to the front door. "He might just be your greatest ally."

"I won't let anything happen to him," Alex said. "You have my word."

Howard extended his hand for a handshake, and Alex accepted it.

"I can't tell you where we're going," Alex said as he started walking back towards the room. "But if you make it out of here, I promise to find you again."

Three shadowy figures appeared in the doorway.

"Go! Now!" Howard shouted with his eyes fixed on the newest arrivals.

Alex hopped over the flames with a renewed sense of urgency. When he made it back to the room, Terry was already standing at the foot of the bed.

"Is my dad coming with us?" Terry asked.

Alex looked crouched down in front of the boy. "We have to go, Terry. Your dad isn't coming with us right now."

Tears welled up in the boy's eyes. He bent down and grabbed the frame of the bed. "Help me move this. Dad told me to use this exit if anything bad ever happened."

Alex nodded. He grabbed the other side of the bed, and together, they moved it off to the side, revealing a trap door. Alex lifted it and helped grab a hold of the ladder below. Once the boy began making his way down, Alex climbed in himself.

He saw shadows that resembled an unfair fight moving around on the wall adjacent to the living room.

That was the last time he saw Howard Lane.

Present Day...

Once all of the adrenaline wore off Kyle began to feel the bumps and bruises that he received from Timmy and general soreness from being on the run all day. He was still in shock about everything that had happened. Not only did he wake up twenty years in the future, but he also had to face off with his younger brother, who was at least a foot taller and robotically enhanced.

As he approached the Medical Bay all he could think about was his mother. He knew that he couldn't trust every word that Timmy said, but if his mom was in trouble he needed to go help her.

"Kyle?" Charlotte popped her head out of her office. "Come on in. You can take a seat in room number two."

Kyle did as he was told, and Charlotte took a look at all of his bumps and bruises. She confirmed what he already knew. He was a little beat up, but overall, he was fine.

"You don't seem to have Russel's accelerated healing," Charlotte.

"Accelerated healing?"

"Yes," Charlotte pushed her glasses up the bridge of her nose. "By the time he arrived here after Lily's rescue mission, his bruises were already on the mend."

"I see," Kyle said.

"How are you feeling?" Charlotte asked with her clipboard in hand.

"I feel fine," Kyle said.

"Can you be honest with me?"

"I guess I feel a little drained."

"That makes sense. You jumped right into a physical confrontation only hours after waking up."

"Listen, I don't have time for all this small talk," Kyle said. "My mother is out there. She needs my help, and I'm sitting here, wasting my time with you!"

"Kyle, calm down," Charlotte said. "I'm just following the standard procedure. You've only been out of the pod a few hours, so I need to keep a close eye on you."

"Like I said, I don't have time for this." Kyle jumped out of the examination table and went straight for the door.

"Where are you going?" Charlotte asked.

"I'm going to find my mother."

———

Russel laid his head down on the pillow and let out a sigh of relief. He didn't get any opportunities to nap, but if one came along then he took it in a heartbeat.

His ribs were bruised, and his back was sore from rolling on the ground and taking punches from that android. Despite the armor, he had a few cuts and scrapes. All things considered; he was lucky. The new generation of androids was bigger, faster, and stronger than anything he'd seen in the past two years. Their upgrades were becoming more and more frequent, and in the back of his mind, he wondered if one day, an android would get the better of him.

He stretched out on his bed as much as his body would allow him to and tried to push the negative thoughts away. He focused on the success of rescuing Lilly and the relief he felt when Kyle stepped in to help fend off the attacker. Having a partner out there meant a lot to Russel. After Alex blew out his knee the year prior, Russel never had a real partner out in the field. Terry did his best, but he was too afraid to get close to any of the androids.

Just as Russel began to feel some relief, the com system in his room went off.

"Russel here. What's going on?"

"We need you to get up to the main level," Alex said. "Right now."

"Did they find us?" Russel sat up and instantly felt it in his ribs.

"No. It's Kyle. He is intending to leave and search for his mother."

"Damn it, Kyle!" Russel stood up. "On my way!"

Kyle stormed past a few dozen people in hallways on his way to the control room. As far as he knew that was the only way out. He was a few doors away from the control when Terry popped out of one of the side doors.

"What are you doing, Kyle?" Terry asked. He positioned himself in the middle of the hallway, blocking Kyle's path.

"I'm going to find my mother," Kyle said. "Now get out of my way."

"You can't do-"

Kyle planted his left foot and used his momentum to kick Terry in the chest, sending the young man tumbling backwards. He landed next to the wall on his knees, coughing and struggling to catch his breath. Kyle stepped over him and continued walking towards the control room.

The few people that remained in the hallway cleared a path for Kyle. He was expecting the entrance to be locked, but the door slid open for him, and he quickly understood why.

Russel was standing at the center of the platform. Kyle had never seen him look more serious.

"I don't know what's gotten into you," Russel said. "But this stops right now."

"I don't have time for this, Russel."

"You're being selfish, Kyle. If you go out there now, you're putting everyone down here at risk."

"Every second I waste here, is another second my mom is in danger out there," Kyle said and began walking towards the platform.

"Alex is a man of his word," Russel stood his ground. "Once the probe comes back, we'll go out there and find your mom."

"I'm not waiting here. Get out of my way, Russel!"

"Fine, we can do this your way." Russel clenched his fist and cracked his neck.

Kyle rolled his eyes before dashing towards Russel and delivering an uppercut aimed right at the pit of his stomach. Russel caught the arm with both hands, pushed him back, and wrapped his arms around Kyle's waist, driving him back and ultimately to the ground.

As Kyle went crashing down to the floor, he wrapped his right arm around Russel's neck, cutting off his air supply. Russel grunted, realizing what was happening; he planted his feet, bent his knees, and threw Kyle over the top, leaving him no choice but to brace for the impact of landing straight on his back.

"Uhhh!" Kyle grunted as landed on the steel platform floor.

Russel rubbed his neck and turned around in time to see Kyle roll to the right and use his arms to drive his body up off the ground.

They were both breathing heavily as they circled each other, looking for a weakness.

"Kyle, this isn't you," Russel said, rubbing his neck.

"You know I don't play well with others. You really thought I was going to just come here, be part of the team, and wait around for orders?" Kyle asked.

"I thought you'd want to help us turn things around after being in hibernation for twenty years," Russel said. "Don't you want to find out why you were put on ice?"

"I can't go back and change what happened!" Kyle shouted.

Kyle charged at Russel with a series of punches. Russel dodged a few of them but caught one right on the chin, which sent him stumbling backwards. Kyle capitalized by delivering a kick to Russel's gut.

It wasn't long before the two of them were rolling around on the floor, trying to get the upper hand.

"I really hoped it wouldn't come to this." Russel blurted out.

"You don't-"

Suddenly, Kyle knew exactly what Russel was doing. He was trying to lock in a sleeper hold.

Kyle had mere seconds before he was out cold. He jerked his head back connecting the top of his head with Russel's chin. The impact wasn't massive, but it gave Kyle the opening he needed to escape Russel's hold and get back on his feet.

Russel rolled to his right and got back on his feet before Kyle could get close.

There were dozens of people around the platform, but no one made a sound.

"You're breathing heavy," Kyle said. "You lucky I'm not in peak condition yet, or you wouldn't have had the chance to put that sleeper hold on me."

Russel ignored the trash talk and kept his eyes focused on Kyle. "Think about what you're doing."

"You can't stop me, Russel! If you're not going to help me, then get out of my way."

The door hissed open once again, and everyone turned their attention to the entrance.

Alex stepped through the doors and glanced down at Terry, who was bent over, holding the wall for support. "Are you alright?" Alex asked.

Terry nodded.

Alex walked right up onto the platform as the young men were tussling for position and revealed a small plastic gun.

"Alex-" Russel began to say while keeping one eye on Kyle.

Alex grabbed Russel by the collar and jerked him back. He pointed the gun at Kyle's leg and pressed the trigger.

The shot was silent, but Kyle collapsed as soon as he felt an impact.

"What the hell was that?" He looked up and yelled from the floor.

"It's a temporary paralyzing agent that Terry and I developed a couple of months ago," Alex said. "You'll be asleep in a matter of seconds."

"You had no right to do that!" Kyle yelled.

"I had every right to do that," Alex said calmly and crouched down. "What you were about to do could endanger every single person down here, and I wasn't about to let that happen."

Kyle wanted to say something back but found his jaw locked, and his eyelids became very heavy.

Terry and Russel stood on each side of Alex with the crowd still surrounding the platform as Kyle began to fall asleep.

"Everyone, please return to your duties," Alex said as he stood back up. He turned to Russel and Kyle. "Carry him to the back room in Charlotte's office."

TEN

"What is your friend's problem?" Terry asked as he barged into the office.

Alex was sitting behind his desk with Russel facing him.

"Terry, are you hurt?" Alex asked.

"I'll be fine once I get some answers," Terry said and walked right up to Russel. "A lot of people risked their lives to obtain Kyle's whereabouts. We didn't go through all of that just to have him running around and attacking people all over the complex.

"I'm sorry it got to this point," Russel sighed. "But I believe Kyle has a point."

"What?" Terry looked over at Alex who didn't seem the least bit surprised.

"Terry," Alex said calmly. "I understand you're upset, and you have every right to be. But why don't you have a seat and let Russel explain?"

"Sure, why not?" Terry said sarcastically and dropped into the chair next to Russel.

"Kyle was never really a team player," Russel began. "He was always more of a lone wolf. What we have here is definitely a team, and he is not used to that. Now, hear me out. Kyle was raised by his mother. When his brother told him that their mom was in danger, that obviously had an effect on him. He was wrong to attack you, Terry, but I think we need someone with his sense of urgency."

"Russel, did you maybe hit your head while the two of you were wrestling in the control room?" Terry asked.

"No," Russel replied, unamused. "How long before the location of the android base is decrypted?"

"Twenty-two hours," Terry said.

"Why are we just sitting around?" Russel looked over at Alex. "We could have gone and checked out the coordinates provided to us by the android."

Alex stroked his beard and shifted his gaze from Russel to Terry. "Russel has a point. We are just sitting around while this woman might be in danger. Yes, the android base is our most important mission, but what separates us from those machines is our compassion."

"I can't believe what I'm hearing," Terry shook his head. "Our drone hasn't shown us anything suggesting that his mom or anyone is being held at that location."

"If someone tipped me off on the location of your father," Alex paused.

"Don't bring my dad into this," Terry said.

"I would have a search party out there immediately," Alex said.

"You're only saying that because you know my father is dead." Terry stood up. "I'm going back to the lab. Good luck on your rescue mission."

Terry slammed the door behind him on the way out.

Alex and Russel exchanged glances, followed by a few seconds of silence.

"You're going to want to go on this mission with Kyle, aren't you?" Alex asked.

Russel nodded in agreement.

"Okay, then I'm going to need you to talk some sense into him," Alex said. "You need to explain to him that you're going with him to find his mom, but once you're back and we have the location of the android base, that mission becomes the priority. Understood?"

"Yes," Russel replied. "I'm not going to talk to him. I know Kyle and I'm not the person he'd want to talk to right now."

"Did you have someone else in mind?"

"I know the perfect person for the job."

"Well, get a move on. Time is ticking, and I need you both back here when that location is decrypted."

———

Kyle woke up with a sore neck, tightness in his throat, and random aches and pains all over his body. All of those things combined did not measure up to the shame that he felt about what took place earlier.

I can't believe I did that to Terry, Kyle thought to himself. *Then I attacked Russel and almost got taken out with my own chokehold.*

He looked up at the dim light above his head. It illuminated the tiny room he was in just enough for him to see that he was alone. There was a steel, black chair next to his bed, but something told him he wasn't going to get visitors anytime soon. It was probably for the best after the way he had acted.

Kyle was about to brush his hair out of his face when he realized that his arms and legs were handcuffed to the bed.

He threw his head back against his pillow and closed his eyes. All he could see were replays of what had happened earlier. He wondered how much time had passed and what would happen to him now that he attacked two key members of this underground society.

What did I do? There is no way they're going to let me go after Mom now.

He remembered his temper flaring up like that when he was younger, but he never physically attacked anyone. Especially not someone he considered a friend like Russel. He wondered if maybe his time in the pod affected his decision-making somehow. Could he no longer be trusted to keep his temper under control?

He hoped that wasn't the case. He always prided himself on keeping a cool head. Even when things got out of hand in the ring, and someone hit him with a stiff punch or kick, he never acted so irresponsibly.

A soft knock on the door interrupted Kyle's train of thought.

Since he couldn't get up to open the door or stop anyone from coming in, he simply called out, "Come in!"

He was convinced it was going to be either Russel or Alex, or maybe both of them, but all of his guesses weren't even close.

A young woman walked inside and avoided all eye contact until she closed the door behind her. She was wearing a white lab coat similar to the one Charlotte wore, and she had her hair tied behind her head in a loose pony tail.

"Hello, Kyle," the young woman said, taking her hands out of her lab coat pockets, and brushing loose strands of hair behind her ears.

Kyle studied her face for a few moments. She looked familiar, but he couldn't quite put a finger on who she was.

"If you don't recognize me, it's okay," she said as if she was reading his mind.

He finally realized who was standing in front of him, but it took him another few seconds to say her name.

"Vanessa?" he finally said. "Is that really you?"

"It's me," she replied and gave him a soft smile.

"I have so many questions," Kyle admitted.

"I know." She grabbed the chair and pulled it as close to the bed as she could before taking a seat. "That's what I'm here for."

Kyle felt a shooting pain in the back of his head. He tried to ignore it, but the pain intensified. He closed his eyes, hoping it would go away, but instead, he began to see flashes of what felt like another life.

He saw himself holding a newborn baby. The image quickly faded, and he saw himself walking in the park, pushing a stroller with a woman by his side. The pain intensified and driving the images out of his head before he could see the woman's face.

He grunted and shook his head. The pain subsided, and he was able to open his eyes.

"Kyle! Are you okay?" Vanessa asked.

"I am. I just have a bit of a headache." Kyle sighed and leaned back against his pillow. "Russel sent you?"

"Russel has spoken to me," Vanessa said. "Alex did too, but I'm not here because of them. I'm here for you."

"How are you even here?" Kyle asked. "You only look a few years older than the last time I saw you. That was twenty years ago."

"Things in Reign got out of control after you disappeared," Vanessa said. "You were one of the first ones. After you, there were a few disappearances a month. The Sheriff said that there would be additional police coming in to patrol the streets, but no one ever came. The last thing I remember is going outside to throw out the trash. Then Alex found me in a pod about four years ago."

"So, it wasn't just Russel and I?" Kyle asked.

"No. By our estimates, there were a little over a hundred kids that disappeared in the year after you went missing," Vanessa said in a somber tone. "Some of us were lucky enough to be rescued by Alex, and later Russel. A lot of the others were experimented on and turned into Androids."

"I didn't realize the extent of it," Kyle looked over at Vanessa.

"Most people don't know the whole story," Vanessa said. "Only those close to Alex know. It helps keep people focused on recovering from that toxin and doing the daily tasks that keep this place running while we search for the android base and hopefully put an end to all of this."

"I see," Kyle said. "What about your parents?"

"From what I know, they left Reign a few months after my disappearance," Vanessa looked down. "I do some undercover work on the surface. I was exposed to the toxin so I'm not able to go on missions like Russel, but I help out where I can."

"I'm sorry," Kyle tried to place his hand on top of hers, but the handcuffs stopped him halfway.

"It's not your fault," Vanessa said and moved her hand close enough for Kyle to reach. "But I'm not the only one. This android takeover needs to be stopped. Russel can't do it on his own. He needs you now more than ever."

"Does he really?" Kyle asked and looked away. All he could think of was how Russel almost put him to sleep in the control room. "He seems to be doing just fine."

"Russel has been beaten within an inch of his life more times than I can remember," Vanessa squeezed his hand. "Everyone that has been rescued over the past two years was brought back here thanks to him."

"So he's got things under control," Kyle insisted. "All I do is get in his way."

"All he's been talking about ever since he's been here is finding you," Vanessa continued. "He believes that the two of you working together can put an end to these androids' control of the city. He thinks that the two of you can infiltrate their base and get the original toxin so we can reverse engineer it and make a cure."

"It sure sounds like he has a lot of faith in me." Kyle felt Vanessa's gaze on him but wouldn't meet it.

"He does. And I do, too." She squeezed his hand softly.

"I think our little encounter in the control room changed things between us," Kyle said. "He won't trust me after that. And I don't blame him."

The door creaked open, and a hooded figure walked in.

"The only thing that's changed are our short-term plans," Russel said as he removed the hood. "Let's get you out of those cuffs and go find your mom."

"How long were you standing out there?" Kyle sat up in his bed.

"Long enough to hear what I needed," Russel shuffled through a set of keys, looking for the ones get Kyle out of his cuffs. "We need to move quickly."

"Russel, listen," Kyle sat up as far as the cuffs would allow. "You don't have to do this. I can go find my mom on my own."

"No, you listen." Russel countered. "We are going to find your mom. Once she is safe, Terry will have the location of the Android base, and you will come with me on that mission and we are going to put an end to the stranglehold that this android program has had on our city."

"Okay, you've got a deal," Kyle said.

"I have a set of armor for you," Russel said. "Just in case we run into any trouble out there."

Vanessa started making her way towards the exit.

"Thank you for taking the time to come down here and talk to me,"

Kyle said. "It almost felt like we were back outside of our lockers for a second."

She gave him another smile. "It did. I hope this isn't the last time we talk."

"It won't be," Kyle said. "As soon as we figure this whole thing out, I'll come find you and take you to another bakery if there are still any open in town."

"Hey guys," Russel stepped in. "I'm a big fan of what's happening here, but if we are going to make this mission happen, we need to leave now."

Vanessa threw her arms around Kyle and hugged him tightly. "Be careful out there."

"Don't worry about me," Kyle said. He wanted to hug her back but couldn't since he was still handcuffed to the bed.

Vanessa took another look at Kyle and gave him a warm smile before exiting the room.

"Let me take these off of you," Russel said and took out a key that unlocked all four of the cuffs. "Here's your armor, too."

"It would have been nice to get unlocked, I don't know, maybe as soon as you walked into the room?" Kyle rubbed his wrists as soon as he was freed and grabbed the armor from Russel and started to put it on quickly. "So, I'm stuck with this color?"

"Terry picks the colors," Russel said. "You get the ugly dark green one, and I have this navy blue one."

"I'm surprised to even get a new armor," Kyle said.

"Terry is a good guy," Russel said. "I didn't expect him to step up to you the way that he did. Even if he did end up with a foot in his chest."

Kyle zipped up his suit. "I'm ready."

———

Alex let the cold water run through his fingers for a few seconds before cupping his hands and splashing some on his face. He looked in the mirror and saw bags under his eyes that were not going away unless he managed to get some sleep.

Sleep wasn't happening for him on this particular night. After two hours of tossing and turning, he decided to abort that mission and found himself fully awake at four in the morning. He wiped his face with a towel and made his way back towards the bedroom. He put on his signature off-duty attire; a loose gray t-shirt with black sweatpants, and headed for the door.

Alex punched in a code, turning the lock mechanism green, and watched the door slide open. The halls were almost completely silent. There was only the buzzing sound coming from the lights on the ceiling. Alex was the only person venturing outside of his room at that time, and he was fine with that. The majority of the underground residents stayed in their quarters after ten o'clock. They would only leave their rooms in case of emergency or if perhaps they couldn't sleep like Alex.

He strolled down the hall at a leisurely pace. For once, there was no imminent mission, no android sightings, and no conflicts between members of his team. He stopped by the cafeteria, the busiest place in the complex outside of the control room. There was no one there, only the lights from the vending machines.

He continued down the hall until he arrived at the elevator. He pressed the button on the wall and waited. When the elevator doors slid open, he stepped right in and clicked the button for the only place that might have another person that was wide awake, just like him.

When the elevator came to a soft halt, Alex stepped out and made his way towards Terry's lab. He punched in another code and watched the door slide open. There was one place that looked exactly the same at all hours of the day and night, and that was Terry's lab. It was completely shrouded in darkness, with the only light emanating from the monitor at the far end of the room.

"Can't sleep, Terry?" Alex asked.

"This decryption is more difficult than I thought," Terry replied without taking his eyes off the monitor. "Also, my ribs are a little sore."

"That's actually why I came down here," Alex said.

"To check on my ribs?"

"No. To talk to you about what happened."

"What happened?" Terry spun his chair to face Alex. "Your newest team member decided to go into business for himself. That's what happened."

"And you didn't hesitate to get in his way," Alex said as he pulled up a chair and sat opposite Terry.

"He is not an android," Terry said. "Maybe it's different."

"No. That's not it." Alex objected. "I think when push comes to shove, you'll forget about what the toxin did to your system. You were afraid, and you disregarded that fear because you knew what was at stake."

"That's not important right now," Terry said. "We are hours away from finding the location of the base, and we don't have a reliable team to execute our most important mission."

"We'll make it work," Alex insisted. "We always did, and we always will."

"That was before you messed up your knee," Terry said. "Without you out there, I don't think Russel can complete the mission. I mean, sure he'll get into the base, and maybe he'll be able to get around a few androids, but you know they've always got a few tricks up their sleeve. We are only getting one shot at this, and I don't feel like we are ready at all."

"Is that why you're up in the middle of the night?"

"That's one of the reasons," Terry admitted. "There is something else."

"What is it?" Alex asked.

"I would rather show you," Terry stood up and walked towards the door on the left side of the room.

"I don't think we've ever used that room before," Alex said as he followed Terry through the entrance.

"Don't freak out," Terry switched on the lights.

Alex waited for his eyes to adjust to the brightness. He was speechless when he realized what he was looking at.

"Well?" Terry asked.

Alex's eyes studied the body that was laid out on the lab table.

It wasn't just any body. It was an android body.

It was confined to the steel table with thick hand and ankle cuffs. It was dressed in a green sleeveless shirt and black shorts. When Alex was able to pry his eyes away from the android, he noticed that there were tools, parts, and monitors scattered all over the room.

"Terry?" Alex shifted his gaze. "Have you been tinkering with this android?"

"More like reprogramming," Terry said with a proud look on his face.

"You didn't think to run this by me?" Alex asked. "You know how dangerous these things are!"

"I know," Terry walked around the lab table. "That's why I kept him here. I installed a device into his neck. If he tries to get past that door, it automatically shuts down all his systems."

"It's still a huge risk," Alex insisted.

"Nothing was working."

"What are you talking about?"

"No matter what treatments Charlotte put me through," Terry looked away. "Nothing was helping me overcome my fear. Especially my fear of these things."

"What's your point?" Alex asked.

"My point is that I used this android to come face to face with what I fear most," Terry said. "I've used it as a sparring partner in this very room. I practiced all of the moves that Russel had taught me over the past couple of years, and I was able to put them to use."

Alex paced around the room slowly while trying to process what was being said. "Is this why you were able to stand up to Kyle?"

Terry nodded.

"I'm glad that you found a way to face your fears," Alex said after some deliberation. "I'm just not okay with you going behind my back to do it."

———

Russel and Kyle agreed to take the armored Jeep for their mission.

The drive began in relative silence until Kyle asked how Russel was driving completely in the dark with no headlights on.

"I got my night vision goggles on," Russel said, prompting Kyle to look over at him. "Push the top three buttons on your wrist console."

Kyle did as he was told, and a pair of goggles emerged from his collar and fixed themselves around his eyes. A few seconds later, he saw the entire street in green and black.

"This armor suit is impressive," Kyle admitted.

"It's the newest model," Russel said. "Let's see how it does out in the field."

Kyle took in as much of his surroundings as he could while Russel sped down what had once been a busy street. There were two wide lanes on each side, and grass separating the road from the sidewalk. Once they got closer to the center of town, Kyle noticed that everything was lit up. There were screens and flashing lights on every store front, and there were lights coming out of every window. People walked up and down the streets but there were no conversations, not even eye contact. Everyone was either looking at a screen on the street or staring directly into their phone.

Russel turned on the lights and reached into the back seat with his free hand. "Here, put on this jacket to cover up your armor and take the night vision goggles off for now."

"Something is off here," Kyle said. He continued to examine the people on the street.

"Take out a phone from the glove compartment and pretend to look at it," Russel said.

"Why?"

"Just do it," Russel said. He slowed down until they were cruising at the same speed as the other cars on the street. "The toxin was just beginning; phase two was the integration of the screens. Everyone is always staring into a computer, a TV, or a screen from the moment they wake up until the moment they go to sleep. It's how they cope with the anxiety induced by the toxin. It also keeps them distracted from their surroundings so they don't realize what's really happening around them."

"This is absolute insanity," Kyle said. He did his best to pretend like he was looking at the phone but his eyes kept darting to the people on the street.

"This is why we need to reverse engineer the toxin," Russel said.

"By our calculation, we only have a few weeks before the damage will become irreversible."

"Why didn't we just do this later at night?" Kyle asked. "When everyone is asleep."

"There is a chance that even more androids will patrol streets at night," Hyden replied. "The only way to get through here is to hide in plain sight."

"Has anyone else we know been turned into an android like my brother?" Kyle asked.

"If we are being honest," Russel kept his eyes fixed on the road. "I don't try to identify them. I try to survive and get away."

"We won't be able to run from them forever, you know."

"I know, but I'm the only one that can go out on these missions."

"That's not true."

"Who else is there?"

"Terry."

"He's probably close, but he's not ready yet."

"He's ready," Kyle said. "I looked into his eyes, and I saw no fear. Just like when I looked into yours before you took me down with my own chokehold."

Russel smirked. "To be fair, it wasn't your chokehold. You learned it from Robert."

"And where did you learn it from?" Kyle asked.

"When I was found, they gave me a few weeks to get acclimated before I was sent out on missions," Russel said. "During that time, I looked up Robert's old instructional videos. I watched every single one, but mainly the conditioning and the self-defense ones."

"Robert was a great teacher," Kyle said somberly. "I wonder if he's still around."

"I looked him up and didn't find anything," Russel said. "I hope he got far away from here before all of this happened."

"I hope you're right," Kyle agreed.

Russel took his foot off the gas and pointed ahead. "That's the old factory right there."

"Good." Kyle's heart began to beat faster with anticipation.

"Before we go in there," Russel began. "Let's get one thing straight.

We are only here for your mom. If we run into your brother, we need to run because it's most likely a trap."

Kyle nodded reluctantly.

"Once Terry gets us the location of their base, we'll be able to help Timmy," Russel brought the car to a complete stop. "That's a promise."

"Okay, let's get in there." Kyle opened the door and hopped out.

Russel locked the car and the two of them met up by the front of the hood.

"Let's keep our eyes open for any movement," Russel whispered. "Since we didn't have time to practice with this armor, I had Terry create a little cheat sheet for you."

"Cheat sheet?"

"Yes. Punch in nine-two-two."

Kyle did as he was told, and a few codes and descriptions popped up in front of his left eye.

"Do you see it?" Russel asked.

"Yes," Kyle said slowly. "This is going to take a little getting used to."

"If we run into the androids, you'll be happy that you have these codes," Russel said and started walking down a brick path that was overgrown by weeds. "Watch your step. I don't see any of them on my radar, but they could be hiding their signatures."

The main entrance to the factory was locked, but Russel had the blueprints downloaded into his armor's memory.

"There is another entrance around the back," Russel said and led the way.

Kyle examined the building as they walked around. There were no signs that anyone was living there, but maybe that was the whole point if his mom was hiding out here.

"This one is locked too," Russel said. "But it's a flimsy lock, so stand back."

Kyle took a step back and watched Russel punch a code into his hand console without looking before ripping the door handle off completely.

"I heated up the lock just enough to rip it off," Russel held up the door handle before tossing it aside into the grass. "Come on in."

Kyle rushed inside and pressed himself against the wall opposite Russel. "What do you see on your console?"

"I see two of them in the building," Russel whispered. "There are two more heat signatures on the second floor."

"One of them has to be my mom," Kyle stuck his head and scanned the hallway. "It's clear."

Russel crouched down and moved down the hall cautiously with Kyle right behind him. They made almost no noise, but once they reached the stairs, that was no longer an option.

"These old stairs are going to creak," Russel whispered.

"We have no choice," Kyle said. "We have to get up there."

"Okay." Russel took a deep breath. "If your mom is here, she'll be in the room at the very end of the hall. There is a good chance we'll run into an android at the top of the stairs. If that happens you let me worry about it. You go get your mom. Understood?"

Kyle nodded, and they started taking careful steps upwards. Each step made a long, drawn-out creaking sound. By the time they made it all the way to the top, they heard loud stomps heading their way.

Russel and Kyle stood back-to-back in the middle of a long hallway.

"Do you see him?" Russel asked.

"No. Can you see where he is coming from on your console?"

"All I see is that he is close!"

"I see him," Kyle said calmly. "Which way is my mom's location?"

"It's this way," Russel said. "Switch positions with me!"

They quickly shifted around just in time for Russel to see the android charging towards him. "I'm going to hold him off until you get your mom. After that it's back to the car. End of the hall, Kyle! Go!"

Kyle pushed off from Russel and ran down the hall as fast as he could.

This wasn't exactly part of the plan, Russel thought as he braced himself for the mountain of a man and machine charging towards him. He bent his knee and darted to the side to avoid a head on collision. The android did not lose his balance as Russel had hoped, but the split second that it took for him to turn around gave Russel the opening that he needed to go on the offensive.

He delivered a hard kick directly towards the android's stomach, driving him back a couple of steps, but he came right back at Russel with an attack of his own.

Even with the armor Russel felt every punch as he tried to cover up and hold his ground.

I really hope Kyle is having better luck than me. Russel ducked and rolled out of the way before regaining his footing and preparing for another showdown.

Kyle reached the end of the hall only to find the door locked. He half expected it. He took a few steps back and kicked the door, instantly loosening up the lock but not quite getting the door to open. Another kick sent the door flying off the hinges and left Kyle standing with one foot in the room.

There was a single bulb providing some dim light and creating a room full of shadows.

"Mom!" Kyle pushed the night vision goggles away from his face. "Are you in here?"

A woman emerged out of the shadows. She was wearing a long brown coat and fuzzy winter hat. She had tiny wrinkles under her eyes and a few around her mouth. The gray hair sticking out from under the hat threw Kyle off a little bit, but once the woman approached the light, everything became clear.

The woman was indeed his mother.

"Mom," Kyle said and staggered forward. He hit the control pad on his wrist and his night vision goggles retracted back into the armor.

Janine did not say a word. She just stared ahead.

"Mom, it's me, Kyle." He took a few more steps forward, but his mom just stood there in silence.

"Mom..."

Russel came crashing through the wall and rolled on the floor right where Kyle was standing.

"Russel!" Kyle shouted and dropped down to check on his friend. "Are you alright?"

"There are new models." Russel winced in pain. "I was doing okay against one, but-"

There was no need to finish the sentence. Three androids walked into the room through the hole in the wall that they had made using Russel's body as a wrecking ball.

"Mom! Stay behind me!" Kyle said, turned to Russel. "I found my mom, so we need to get out of here."

The androids stood still on opposite sides of the whole in the wall.

"What's going on?" Kyle asked. "Why aren't they moving?"

"Kyle," Russel's voice trailed off as he got back on his feet. He looked past his friend.

Kyle looked back at his mom, and his heart stopped.

The fuzzy hat and coat were gone. Replaced by dirty rags. She had a blank stare; her cheeks were sunken, and her teeth were all missing.

The walking corpse that was standing in front of Kyle collapsed on the ground.

"Mom!" Kyle shouted. He dropped to the ground and picked up her head gently with two hands. He brought her into his chest and hugged her. "Stay with me, Mom! We are going to get you help."

Russel walked over and put his hand on Kyle's shoulder. He wasn't sure what else to do.

Russel heard a creaking sound from the opposite end of the room as if someone had stood up from an old chair. "Who is there?"

That part of the room was completely shrouded in darkness.

Another android stepped into the room through the hole in the wall.

Kyle recognized the middle android almost instantly. "Timmy?"

"That's not Timmy," said the man in the shadows. "That model number seven-four-one. He is a state-of-the-art android unit. Very obedient, but he retained his human qualities to help with missions such as this one."

Kyle helped Russel up to his feet and said: "Why don't you come on out so we can see who we're dealing with?"

"Now would be as good a time as any, I suppose."

The man stepped out of the shadows, revealing a clean shaved head and a contrasting thick, black beard. He was dressed in the same attire as the androids, but he was clearly human.

Kyle and Russel let out a collective gasp.

"It can't be," Russel murmured. "Dad? Is that really you?"

Felix smiled and reached out his right hand towards his son. "Let's go Russel. You've wasted enough time with these people."

"I'm not going anywhere with you until I get some answers," Russel looked around the room. "Until we both get some answers."

"I don't owe him any explanations," Felix said. "But I do have big plans for you."

Russel shook his head.

"Don't make this difficult," Felix said and let out a sigh. "Don't make me have to get these androids to drag you out of here."

"Are you one of them?" Russel asked. He shifted his gaze from the androids to his father, searching for similarities.

Felix let out a short laugh. "One of them? No. They are my loyal servants. They do as I say. That's how I was able to take control of this good for nothing town."

"I don't believe it. So you're responsible for everything that happened, Dad?"

"I am the architect of everything that's happened! And it all happened because of you!" Felix pointed at Kyle. "You had my son hopping around that ring like some kind of circus clown. And you're the reason he broke his neck!"

"You're out of your mind," Kyle said just loud enough for everyone to hear. "You turned this town into a big experiment. You experimented on my *mom!*"

"Perhaps I did," Felix said with a smug look on his face. "The experiment with your mom was clearly a failure, but she came in useful here, did she not? Outside of this little group of rebels, everyone is living happily in Reign."

"You'll pay for what you did!" Kyle interjected.

"You are partially responsible for everything that's happened in this town, young man," Felix raised his eyebrows at Kyle.

"And how is that?"

"You are the reason my son found himself at death's door. That's when I realized that none of my work meant anything if I couldn't keep my son safe. I agreed to be a host, of sorts, for this experiment. When I saw how well it was doing, I took the lead. That's how we ended up with the paradise you see yourself surrounded with today."

"Dad," Russel took two steps forward. "What paradise? The people of Reign are scared of their own shadows. They are terrified of being snatched up by one of your androids. Look what you did to this poor woman!"

"It's a small price to pay for a peaceful existence," Felix said calmly.

The consoles on Kyle's and Russel's arms let off a soft vibration, but it was enough to draw their attention away from Felix for just a moment.

It was a message from Terry. He finally broke through the encryption and found the location of the android base. Russel looked over at Kyle, hoping he saw it too but his gaze was fixed on his mother's lifeless body.

"What's the matter?" Felix asked. "You two got somewhere to be?"

"Dad, you have to put a stop to this," Russel pleaded. "This is madness."

"Put a stop to this?" Felix began to laugh. "This is only the beginning. You're going to help me see this all the way through."

Russel walked over to Janine and felt for a pulse. He looked over at Kyle and shook his head. "I'm so sorry, Kyle. But we need to go."

Russel helped Kyle up off the floor.

"You're not going anywhere!" Felix said sternly. "You think you're going to return to that precious underground base of yours? I have ten units similar to the ones you see here on the way to infiltrate your base. In about thirty minutes, there will be nothing left."

"You can't do that!" Russel shouted. "We've got innocent people there! Women and children on the road to recovery from the toxin!"

"It's not a toxin!" Felix's eyes grew wide with anticipation. "It's a cure! And don't you worry, my son. We've got plans in place for every single resident of that not-so-secret-place."

"We need to go, Kyle," Russel said. "They don't stand a chance without us."

"I see you're not going to come peacefully," Felix said.

Kyle and Russel did their best, but they were no match for three androids.

Kyle was completely numb. He saw the punches and the kicks hit his body. He tasted the blood in his mouth but didn't feel a thing.

One of Timmy's blows sent him flying into the wall. He watched the other two androids drag Russel out of the room. Timmy bent down to pick up Kyle.

"Stop," Felix ordered. "He deserves to lay here and think about all of the lives that he ruined. Leave him."

The last thing Kyle saw before blacking out was Felix and Timmy storming out of the room. He could not bring himself to look at his mom's lifeless body again.

ELEVEN

"**A**ttention Everyone! This is not a drill! Red Alert! Please evacuate the premises!"

Alex hoped he'd never hear that message over the loudspeaker. He stood up and made his way towards the door. He swung it open and found the residents of his complex rushing towards the stairways.

Terry popped out of the sea of people. "I just saw the cameras. There are two androids breaking through the control room platform. Four more pairs are coming in from different directions."

Alex took a deep breath. He grabbed Terry by the elbow, led him into the room, and closed the door behind them.

"Kyle and Russel aren't here," Alex said.

"They could not have picked a worse time." Terry shook his head.

"I sent out an alert. For now, it's just you and me." Alex rushed over to the monitor at his desk and flipped it around for Terry. "We can take these two in the control room, Terrance. Are you up for it?"

"Yes," Terry said convincingly.

"Suit up." Alex flipped the screen around. I'll meet you in the control room in two minutes."

———

"How much time do you need?" Alex asked outside the Medical Bay's doors checking to make sure he put his armor on correctly.

"I'll need at least fifteen minutes," Charlotte said. She was darting from one side of the room to the other, trying to prepare all four of her patients for transport.

"We'll give you fifteen minutes," Alex said confidently and began to walk off when Charlotte grabbed his arm.

"You shouldn't be doing this. Your leg isn't fully recovered."

"I have to do this. Otherwise, they'll run right through this place."

"Where are Russel and Kyle?"

"Not sure. My guess is the mission to find Kyle's mother did not go according to plan."

"Be careful out there," Tears welled up in Charlotte's eyes.

"Get these people to safety," Alex said and softly places his hands on Charlotte's shoulders. "You can do this. I'll see you at the rendezvous point."

———

Terry waited by the entrance to the control room. He could hear the androids breaking through the locking mechanism on the control room platform. It was only a matter of time before they broke through. Minutes. Perhaps even seconds.

Terry's armor was on, and all of the latest gadgets were in place. He wasn't worried about any of those. The only thing he was actually worried about was his most important gadget.

He rubbed his temples.

If his mind wasn't right, it didn't matter how many androids came down through the platform. He'd be absolutely useless. But his mind *needed* to be right. With Russel nowhere to be seen, he and Alex were the only two people standing between the androids at the evacuation routes.

He couldn't let Alex down, not after everything they had been through together.

The elevator doors slid open, and Alex emerged wearing his burgundy armor. He was doing his best to hide his limp, but Terry knew that his mentor was far from fighting shape. He also knew that wasn't going to stop him.

"I made sure to give you extra padding and support for that right leg of yours," Terry said as Alex approached.

"Thank you" Alex said and joined his protege at the entrance to the control room. "It feels great."

"Did you memorize all of the commands?"

"I memorize them all any time you update them."

"So, every week, you sit there and memorize the entire list?"

"Yes."

"Why?"

"Look at our predicament, Terry. They already have so many advantages over us. They are faster, and stronger, they don't feel pain, and they'll stop at nothing to complete their mission. The last thing I want to do is make it easier for them to take me down because I don't remember the command that might be effective at stopping them."

"I made sure to limit their advantages as much as possible," Terry said and looked up at the ceiling. "They're almost in."

"It's alright," Alex said. His eyes were fixed on the ceiling as well. "If they think they are just going to walk past us without a fight, they've got another thing coming."

"We've got about twenty minutes to deal with them," Terry said, looking at his console. "There is another batch not far behind them."

"Let's deal with them one wave at a time," Alex said. "By holding these two off for at least fifteen minutes, we'll give Charlotte and her patients enough time to escape."

They watched as some debris began to fall from the ceiling. The locking mechanism was failing, and the platform was becoming loose. More debris was followed by a loud thud and a slow descent by the platform down into the control room. Two long shadows extended out towards Alex and Terry. The androids stood on the opposite side of the platform. Their all-black uniforms were covered in dust, but their clean-shaven heads reflected the lights directly behind them.

"This is what you've been preparing for, Terrance," Alex said and started walking confidently towards the platform. "Let's show them what we've got."

Terry didn't know if what he was seeing was the product of Alex's adrenaline, his adrenaline, or perhaps both. But the limp was completely gone.

Alex marched in to face the intruders head on.

Terry took a deep breath and made his way towards the platform, which was about half way down. The androids stood completely still. As usual they displayed no signs of emotion. Terry met Alex at the foot of the platform.

"My heart is beating really loud," Terry said.

"So is mine," Alex replied. "And it's completely okay."

———

"Dad! Wake up!"

Kyle opened his eyes and found himself on the living room couch. He jumped up off the couch and looked around frantically.

How can this be possible? None of this was real.

"What's wrong, dad?"

"Kevin?" Kyle took a few steps back from his son. "What's happening here?"

Kevin looked up at Kyle and tugged on the side of his pants. "Are you feeling okay, Dad?"

"I'm not sure buddy," Kyle said, and for a moment, he decided that he did not care if it was real or not. He bent down and hugged his son. "I missed you, Kevin."

"I missed you too Dad," Kevin said and stretched his little arms around his dad's back as far as he could. "And I wish you could stay here with me and maybe go upstairs and play with my new action figures."

"That would be great, wouldn't it?"

"But you can't stay here, Dad."

"Why is that, Kevin?"

"We both know why."

"I don't know what I'm supposed to do," Kyle said and walked back over to the couch.

"The same thing you always told me to do," Kevin plopped himself on the couch next to his dad. "Always do the right thing."

"I'm no match for those androids," Kyle admitted.

"Those people need your help," Kevin said. "You can't just sit here with me on this imaginary couch."

"Imaginary? Kyle asked.

"You know this isn't real, Dad," Kevin said with a serious look on his face. One that Kyle had never seen before. "You need to go and help those people so nobody else ends up like grandma!"

Kyle opened his eyes and instantly felt pain shooting down his back and legs. He looked down at his wrist and found it vibrating with big, bold letters that said; *Red Alert. All Units Report back to the base!*

He wiped the blood from the side of his mouth, brushed his hair out of his face, and used the wall for support to stand up. He took one last look at his mom. "They will pay for this, mom. I promise."

————

After their arrival at Coleman Tech Tower, Russel was given a suite to clean himself. He was escorted to his father's meeting room shortly after.

"You disappoint me, Russel," Felix said with his back turned and his hands folded behind his back. "I expected you to see things my way."

"I can't see things your way until you stop this madness," Russel said and looked back at the three androids behind him.

"If only you had remained in the pod until I retrieved you," Felix said. He looked down and shook his head in disappointment. "Things would have been so different."

"Different how? Would you have turned me into one of these things behind me?"

Felix turned around with a raised eyebrow. "Never! These things are a means to an end. You are supposed to be their leader. Reign was meant to be your training ground before taking over the surrounding cities!"

"What are you talking about?" Russel asked. "I'm not taking over anything! I'm twenty years old, and I spent the past two decades floating around in a pod!"

"It was all part of the plan after you nearly died!" Felix shouted. He turned around to face his son. "I gave you too much freedom and not enough guidance. I spent the last twenty years fixing that. I changed this whole town in order to make sure no other parent would ever have to go through what I went through. Yes, their freedom is a bit limited. I'm not blind to that, but I provided everyone with what they need to keep themselves safe."

"Dad," Russel said softly. "What happened to me was an accident. I landed wrong. It could have happened to anyone."

"I know," Felix said. The rage had disappeared from his voice. "I created a world where things like that don't have to take place. What happened to you will never happen to anyone again."

Russel took a few steps back. "I'm not going to help you, Dad."

"I've learned a lot of things in our time apart," Felix said. "One of those things is that some people thrive when they have plenty of choices. Others need their choices to be limited."

"What are you saying?"

"I'm saying you belong to the second group." Felix looked past his son. "Take him away."

"Wait! Dad! You can't do this!" Russel protested as two androids grabbed him on each side and began to drag him out of the room.

"That's where you're wrong son," Felix said with a grin. "In this town, I can do whatever I want."

———

Alex and Terry engaged the androids as soon as they stepped off the platform. The initial adrenaline rush gave them the upper hand early on, but the androids' ability not to get tired took its toll.

Alex kept himself in good shape for his age, but his body wasn't ready to take on an android. He did his best to hold his own, but it was only a matter of time before the android got the better of him.

On the other side of the control room Terry was having his own struggles. He was having a hard time catching his breath from the moment he caught a glimpse of the androids coming down the control room platform. He was defending himself very well, but they needed more than defense if they were going to survive this onslaught.

"Alright, kid! What do we have for these brutes?" Alex asked from across the room. "How about one-one-three?"

"Punch it in!" Terry shouted while dodging punches. "Then step back and point both arms up at his face!'

Alex did as he was told and saw a green mist shoot out of his wrist area into the android's face.

"It blinds them!" Terry shouted again, "At least for a few moments."

Alex took advantage of the opening that was provided to him. He ducked down to avoid the android's arm and ran directly towards his waist. He wrapped his arms around the android and used every ounce of strength he had left to lift him off the ground and slam him onto the floor.

The disoriented androids flailed his arms and legs on the ground until Alex used another command to glue his arms and legs down to the ground. Alex took a step back and punched in a third command into the console. This one pinpointed the exact location that needed to have an electric current run through it in order to disable the android. He followed the instructions, and a few seconds later, the battle was over. The android was fully deactivated.

Terry followed similar steps to bring his opponent down, and when it was done, the two of them met in the center of the room.

"Those were older models, weren't they?" Alex asked when he got close enough not to have to shout.

"Definitely," Terry rested his hands on his knees while breathing heavily. "We got very lucky. The next wave will not be as easy, and they are only seven minutes away."

———

Russel stood in a tight elevator next to his father, surrounded by the three androids. He figured there was no point in trying to escape. The three androids had apprehended him already, and he knew he wasn't going to outrun them inside their own base.

The elevator came to a halt, and the doors slid open. Felix didn't say anything to the androids but they somehow knew to exit the elevator and go left.

Felix and Russel went in the opposite direction.

The floors were made out of white marble, while the walls were painted in a contrasting gray. There were no windows and barely any doors. There was no one in the hall besides them, and that threw Russel off. He was used to the tight, crowded halls of Alex's complex.

"Where are we going?" Russel asked impatiently.

"We are going to the lab for some adjustments," Felix replied without looking at his son.

"Adjustments?"

"You'll see."

They arrived at a lab that resembled Terry's lab but somehow darker, even though there were dozens of screens along the walls and perfectly lined up desks. There were people working behind each desk, but no one paid any attention when Felix and Russel entered the room.

"They're all androids, aren't they?" Russel asked.

"Yes," Felix replied. "They are the perfect workers. They follow their job descriptions, they don't ask any questions, and they never need to take a break."

"How do they know what to do? Who controls them?" Russel asked as they approached something that looked like a combination between an advanced video game chair and a dentist's chair.

"It's all up here," Felix tapped the side of his head with his index finger. "They are all connected to me. Nothing they do happens without me knowing."

Russel took a closer look at where his father was tapping. He could see a circuit board of some sort attached to his skin under the stubble on his head. He had never seen anything like it before, not even on the androids themselves.

"Take a seat," Felix put one hand on his son's shoulder. "We'll get you one of these, and in a few hours, you'll have an army of androids at your command."

Russel turned and took a big step back away from his dad. "Whoa, Dad! I never agreed to that!"

"You silly kid," Felix smirked. "Your days of agreeing with what I have planned for you are over. You're going to do what I say, or you'll end up just like your buddies in the complex, as one of the casualties."

"Don't you dare hurt those people!" Russel said and pointed at his dad. "There are innocent people down there. They deserve a chance to live how they want to live. They deserve to make their own decisions. No one wants to be a robot like these poor souls that you've enslaved here."

"You don't know what you're talking about," Felix said, unamused. "Everyone in Reign is happier than they've ever been. Outside of the activity of your friends, we haven't had any crimes in nearly fifteen years."

"You've had people living in a trance that whole time," Russel insisted. "It's not something to be proud of."

"I see how this is going to go," Felix said. The smirk returned to his face. "Strap him in."

A new group of androids emerged out of the shadows and grabbed Russel. They carried him to the chair with ease despite his struggles. Before he knew it, he was strapped in and unable to move.

"They are going to stop you," Russel said.

"There is going to be no one left to stop me," Felix said confidently. "In about an hour, that base will be burned down. There will be no trace of it. And by the time I'm done with the survivors it won't even be a memory."

TWELVE

K yle gripped the wheel so tight that his hands and shoulder began to ache. He ignored the pain and hit the gas. He did not concern himself with keeping a low profile and raced through the streets, which were now completely dark. Everything was turned off, and there were no people outside. Kyle felt like he was driving through an abandoned amusement park.

The thought of androids following him back to the hideout briefly crossed his mind, but he didn't care. Felix already had androids on the way, and Kyle had no time to waste.

His thoughts kept going back to his mother.

How long was she there? What if I got there sooner?

He shook his head and picked up more speed. He was no longer concerned about how many androids were waiting for him. He was going after them with everything he had.

Kyle got as close to the platform as he could and jammed the brakes forcing the car to slide for a few feet. He hopped out and punched in his code to reveal the platform. He hopped on and paced anxiously for what seemed like an eternity as the platform lowered him down into the control room.

As he got close to the bottom, he saw Alex laying on the floor motionless with an Android stomping away from his body to the opposite side of the control room. Kyle followed the android's trajectory and spotted Terry on the opposite side of the room, trying to fend off another android.

Kyle's heart began to beat faster, and he clenched his fists.

"Come on, come on!" He yelled at the platform. He did not wait for it to reach the bottom. He jumped off as soon as it was close enough for him to do so.

He landed on both feet, ran towards Alex, and bent down to check if he was alive.

"Help... Terry," Alex murmured with one eye open.

"Hey!" Kyle shouted in the android's direction. "Your fight is with me now!"

The android did not acknowledge him and stayed on course.

This made Kyle even angrier. He charged at the android at maximum speed and lunged directly at the back of his knees, sending the android folding backward. Kyle used his arms to push himself back up and jumped on top of his enemy pummeling him with both fists.

The android managed to push Kyle off with relative ease, which gave him enough time to roll out of the way and get back on his feet. Kyle did not relent; he attacked with a series of uppercuts and a knee to the midsection, driving the android back.

"Fighting an able-bodied man is not part of your programming?" Kyle yelled as he knocked the android off of his feet for the second time. The android got up on one knee, but Kyle used the rigid sole of his boot to kick him directly in the face, sending him back down to the floor. His fingers fumbled around the keypad on his armor for a few seconds, but he eventually found the code for the electric cuffs and used it to tie down the hands and knees of his adversary.

Convinced that this android was no longer a threat, Kyle shifted his attention toward Terry. Judging by the black and blue under his right eye and the multiple cuts on his face, he had taken quite a beating.

Kyle stayed low to the ground and hid behind the row of computers as he approached the android from behind. Once he was within striking distance, he wrapped his arm tight around the android's waist, popped his hips, and used every ounce of strength to lift him off the ground before slamming him down on his face.

Terry fell back against the wall and attempted to catch his breath. He wiped some blood off his face and watched as Kyle and the android wrestled on the ground, trading vicious blows to the head.

Terry pushed up off the wall and stumbled toward Alex, who was still laying exactly where Kyle found him. "Charlotte! Come in! Alex is down!" He hoped that Charlotte was somewhere close by and able to hear him.

Kyle continued his fight with the androids. He knew he was getting hit harder than ever before but he didn't feel the pain. Each blow he received only made his own punches stronger. He managed to push the android back against the wall and continued to deliver punch after punch even after it became clear that the android was unable to defend himself.

Charlotte and Vanessa ran into the room. Charlotte was carrying a first aid kit. "Stop him! It's over!" she said and motioned for Vanessa to go to Kyle while Charlotte tended to Alex.

"Kyle, stop!" Vanessa shouted. Once she was close enough, she tried to grab one of his arms, but he escaped her grip with minimal effort and delivered another strong blow to the head. "Kyle, stop!"

Vanessa ran in front of Kyle and dropped down next to the android. "Kyle... Please."

This time, he listened. The attack ceased, and he pushed the android off to the side.

"She's gone," Kyle whispered. He sat down on the floor next to Vanessa. "I was too late."

"I'm so sorry," Vanessa said and put her arm around Kyle bringing him closer to her.

"She died right in front of me," Kyle said as tears welled up in his eyes.

Vanessa hugged him even tighter.

"Where is Russel?" Terry asked from across the room.

"He was taken," Kyle stood up. "It was a trap."

"I told you!" Terry yelled. "But you didn't want to listen!"

Kyle did not argue. "His father is behind all of this."

"Felix?" Alex struggled to his feet with an assist from Charlotte.

"Alex, you need to take it easy," Charlotte said.

"This is not the time to take it easy dear," Alex said. "Felix is alive?"

The five of them met in a circle where Alex and Charlotte were standing.

"He was behind it all," Kyle said. "Everything that happened in Reign in the last twenty years was set up by him. The toxin, the androids, the lockdown. It's all him."

"I thought you said he disappeared years ago," Terry said. "How can this be?"

"I don't know Terry," Alex said. "We'll have to deal with this later. As of right now we got four more androids coming this way."

Everyone except Kyle frowned at Alex's remark. "Let them come," he said and started walking back towards the platform.

Terry shook his head while the other exchanged looks of concern.

Alex let go of Charlotte and limped over to Kyle.

"I heard about your mother," Alex said once he was only a few feet behind Kyle. "I'm really sorry. I wish we had found her sooner."

Kyle remained silent. There was nothing anyone could do now.

"Russel is with his father?" Alex asked.

"Yes."

"I'm going after him."

"You're in no shape to go after anyone."

"I have no choice."

"We'll go together," Kyle said and looked over at Alex. Then looked back at Terry who was only a few feet behind them. "All of us. We owe that much to Russel."

"I need about twenty minutes to patch up our suits," Terry said.

"Don't forget mine," Vanessa said as she walked up to join the others.

"She is trained," Alex said. "And we did have one made for her specifically for times like these. However, Vanessa, I need you to take the sewer shuttle back to your hub and prepare for the final phase of the mission. I'll meet you there once we regroup here."

"While Terry patches up the suits, Alex, you need to get patched up with Charlotte," Kyle said. "We are going to need you on this next mission."

"The next batch of androids is about forty minutes away," Terry said. "That should give us enough time to get ready and be gone before they get here."

———

Russel entered a vast space that he could only describe as a throne room. The walls were lined with windows and cushioned benches. At the center of the far end of the room, there was a set of steps that led up to a very comfortable-looking throne. A huge, round lamp hung down from the ceiling illuminating the center of the room, while smaller lights set up the ambiance for the rest of the room, as well as, a set of metal sliding doors on each side.

"What is this place?" Russel asked.

"This is where I make my most important decisions son," Felix replied. "Bring him out!"

Russel looked around to see who his father was talking to but saw no one. Felix left his son standing under the spotlight in the middle of the room while he made his way up to his throne. He plopped down, leaned back, and crossed his legs as he sank into the cushions.

Russel opted not to ask any more questions. He took a deep breath and waited patiently. It took a few moments for the door to his right to slide open. Russel could never have guessed the identity of the person who emerged from those doors.

He was a few inches taller than Russel, with more muscle definition, and buzzcut. But there was no denying the identity.

Russel was standing across the room from *himself.*

"Dad, what in the world is going on here?" Russel asked. He glanced over at Felix, who had an amused smirk plastered all over his face.

"What's wrong?" He asked. "You don't like what you see?"

"It's not about what I like," Russel muttered. "I just don't understand why."

"Because I'm no longer in the business of taking chances," Felix said, instantly erasing the smirk from his face. "There was no guarantee that you would come out of that pod one hundred percent functional. I had to have a contingency plan. You're looking at him. A clone of you, my son, with a few alterations. He's never asked me any questions, he doesn't have any ethical concerns as you've always had, and most importantly, he's ruthless. It's a characteristic I had hoped you would develop over time, but it never happened. At this point, I'm not sure it ever will."

"So now that you have us both here," Russel said and looked into the eyes of his clone. He no longer needed a verbal explanation. He knew exactly what would happen next. He took a few steps forward, put his right hand up in front of his chest, and motioned for the clone to bring it.

"You catch on quick," Felix said and sat back down. "Now, let's see which one of you will be at my side during my conquest."

Something isn't right here, Russel thought as he prepared to collide with an opponent who was charging at him. *My Dad would never go this far. Or would he?*

The clone lunged at Russel with cat-like quickness even though he was at least twenty pounds heavier. Russel side stepped him and delivered a series of punches to his face and torso. The clone was caught off guard but recovered quickly and went on the offensive. Russel ducked a few punches, but got caught with a strong kick to the stomach that sent him stumbling back towards the wall.

Felix's eyes darted from his son to the clone as they exchanged blows.

Russel tried to sweep the bigger man off his feet, but was unsuccessful. Instead, he found himself getting pulled into a bear hug.

This isn't good at all. He felt himself being pulled by the foot with relative ease. *He's a lot stronger than me.*

Doubt started to creep into his mind, but Russel blocked it out. Once the clone pulled him close enough, he flipped over onto his back and kicked him right in the face, loosening his grip in the process. He scurried away from his opponent, who was visibly upset by the unexpected kick.

"Very impressive, Russel," Felix shouted from the throne with a hint of surprise.

"You're sick, Dad," Russel yelled back. "You need help! You cloned your own son!"

"You'll be the one who needs help if you don't pay attention," Felix said just loudly enough for his son to hear him.

Russel shifted his gaze back to his opponent just in time to see a fist flying at him. He put up his arms to block it but was sent flying towards the wall anyway. He felt his back and head slam against the wall and then he slid down to the floor.

The last thing Russel saw was the clone's boot flying towards his face.

———

Terry collected everyone's suits and took them down to his lab while Charlotte escorted Alex back to the Medical Bay for treatment.

Kyle and Vanessa were left alone in the control room with not much to do but wait. Relaxing seemed like an odd thing to do at a time like this, but Kyle and Vanessa sat down across from each other at one of the few tables that was not damaged.

"Are you okay?" Vanessa asked after a few minutes of silence.

"It's just a few bumps and bruises," Kyle said. "I'll be fine."

"I'm not just talking about that."

"If things don't go exactly as planned on this mission. I need you to do me a favor."

"What do you -?"

"Retrieve my mom's body and give her a proper funeral."

"Okay," Vanessa said. She reached across the table and took Kyle's hand. "Hopefully, everything goes as planned."

"I'm not so sure," Kyle said and pulled his hand back. "I'm sorry."

"It's okay."

"Can I ask you something?"

"Sure."

"Do you remember anything from when you were in stasis?"

"Not really. I remember looking back at my house with the moon in the background. Next thing I knew Alex was helping me out of that tank."

"I see," Kyle said and looked away.

"You remember something," Vanessa said.

"I don't think I should tell you."

"You were never big on sharing, but why don't you give it a shot?"

"I lived a whole life in that tank," Kyle began but struggled to maintain eye contact.

"Kyle," Vanessa said. "It's alright. Tell me."

"You were there," Kyle said and forced himself to look up. "We were married, we had a house. And we had a little ten-year-old boy... Kevin."

Vanessa listened but did not interrupt.

"Everyone was so happy," Kyle continued. "Then I woke up to this nightmare only to find out that none of that was real."

"It's not fair," Vanessa spoke up. "None of this should have happened."

"We have to put a stop to Felix's sick experiment on this town and its people."

"We will," Vanessa said with a hopeful smile. "You still have to take me to a bakery, remember?"

For a moment, Kyle felt like he was back at his locker with Vanessa, but the feeling faded quickly.

"The suits are ready," Terry said as soon as the doors hissed open.

Kyle and Vanessa stood up and prepared to make their way towards Terry when the platform began to descend again.

"What's happening?" Kyle asked.

Vanessa pushed past some chairs and turned on the closest computer. "There are four of them on that platform!"

"Oh crap!" Terry said. He dropped the suits and ran back down the hall.

"Terry!" Kyle yelled. His eyes darted back to the platform, where he saw four sets of boots. "Vanessa, get back!"

Vanessa ran to the door, grabbed Kyle's suit and threw it to him. "Put this on quickly."

"There is not enough time," Kyle said, his eyes still fixed on the platform. "Make sure Alex and Charlotte are out of here. I'll hold them off."

"Kyle -"

"Vanessa, go!" Kyle shouted. "There is no time!"

She ran for the door as Kyle prepared to face four androids dressed in pair of sweatpants and an undershirt.

He looked at the suit lying next to him and retrieved the electric baton.

Better than nothing.

He activated the baton just in time for the platform to stop. The androids looked at him and stepped off the platform in perfect synchrony.

There were two rows of computers, tables, and chairs separating the androids from Kyle. With no time to waste, Kyle grabbed the chair closest to him and threw it in the android's direction. The force of his throw made the android take one step back before he tossed the chair aside.

Kyle walked down the aisle way, pushing tables and chairs forward in an attempt to prevent the androids from surrounding him.

They moved slowly and strategically in an attempt to corner him until one of them jumped up on a table and lunged at Kyle. He jumped out of the way and activated his baton in time to hit the android on the back of the head as soon as he landed. The electric shock at the impact sent him tumbling into the mess of monitors, chairs, and laptops.

Kyle shifted his attention to the other three who paid their fallen ally no mind. They had their sights fixed on Kyle.

This is good, Kyle thought. *It will give the others time to escape.*

The remaining three picked up the pace, and Kyle saw all three of them coming at him at the same time. He dodged their attacks as best he could, but it did not take long for them to land a blow that sent him to the ground.

He landed with a thud and instantly regretted not having the armor on. He jumped back up on his feet only to be pummeled all over again with a frenzy of punches and kicks, leaving him gasping for breath on the floor.

His vision became blurry but he did hear loud footsteps coming from the entrance to the control room. He was expecting another attack when one of the androids fell on the floor next to him, and the other two turned around to defend themselves.

"Kyle! Get up! We have to run!" Terry grabbed Kyle by his right arm and pulled him up off the floor.

"Nice of you to show up," Kyle said and looked back at the fight behind him. "What's happening? I only see androids."

"I'll explain later," Terry said as they reached the door. He handed Kyle his suit. "Hold on to this, please."

Kyle grabbed the suit and leaned on the wall in the hallways for support.

"Time to go!" Terry yelled.

"Terry, he is coming right for us!" Kyle yelled as an android ran through the door, and it hissed and closed behind him. He prepared to defend himself, but to his surprise, the android did not attack him. He stood there while Terry punched in a code to lock the door.

"Good job Vince," Terry said and patted the android on the back.

"I'm confused," Kyle said. His eyes darted from Terry to the nearly six foot six, bald mountain of a man with android armor.

"Kyle, meet Vince," Terry said. "He's a reprogrammed android."

———

Alex's jeep was already running when Kyle, Russel, and Vince jumped in the back seat.

Alex hit the gas as soon as the doors were shut, but he kept glancing back at Vince.

"You are not happy about my presence here," Vince pointed out.

"I'm not," Alex said. "What gave it away?"

"I assure you Terry reprogrammed and tested me thoroughly," Vince said.

"That doesn't mean I'm going to trust you," Alex said.

Terry cleared his throat. "Time is of the essence here," he said. "And we need all of the help we can get."

"Where are Vanessa and Charlotte?" Kyle asked.

"Vanessa raced back to her cabin in the woods," Alex said. "There is sensitive information on a hard drive there that needs to be wiped before we can proceed with our mission. Charlotte left to rejoin the others. There were a few injuries during the evacuation."

"Are you feeling up to doing your part of the mission?" Terry asked.

"What do I always say, Terry?" Alex asked.

"We rest at the end. Never in the middle." Terry rolled his eyes.

Satisfied with the boy's answer, Alex asked, "What do we have, kid?"

Terry hit a few buttons on his wrist and pulled up a map, which loaded up onto the car's dashboard. "We have their location. It's up in the mountains, but it's not impossible to get to."

"There are no cameras or guards at the gate," Vince said. "Once the toxin was distributed to the public, there was no need for them."

"We'll break in here," Terry pointed to the front entrance. "Then we'll split up to cover more ground. Our main objective is to destroy their control center. If Vince's programming still applies, which I'm fairly certain that it does, then once we destroy the control center the androids will stop their current behavior."

"Do we know exactly where the control room is?" Kyle asked.

"We do not," Terry replied but pointed down at the map. "I suspect it's here, but I think we'll find it once we get inside. It's not something any of us will miss."

"What about the others?" Kyle asked. "Like my brother and ones like him?"

"It's taken care of," Alex glanced over to Terry.

"Part of the programming to stop the control center functions will place tracking devices on all of the androids connected to that network," Terry said.

"When the dust settles, we'll find you brother, and the others," Alex said reassuringly. "We are not going to abandon anyone. We're going to see this thing through."

Kyle nodded. "Okay then."

Wait," Vince spoke up. "There is one very important person that you've left out of your plan."

"Who is that?" Alex asked.

"The Overseer."

"Is that what you call him? Felix isn't going to do any of his dirty work," Alex said with confidence. "That's why he has so many androids running around."

"You cannot underestimate him," Vince insisted. "Felix is not the man that you knew all those years ago. He has changed."

"What do you mean by that?" Kyle asked.

"I was there early on," Vince said. "The Android Program was just one of the many experiments that were being conducted there. There were a lot of things happening. One of them was a portal that Okada managed to open. It was into some kind of parallel dimension. That's where they got all of this advanced technology from so quickly."

"A parallel dimension," Alex said slowly as he searched his memory. "Now that you said that, it does ring a bell. I remember Felix and Okada discussing something about a parallel dimension, but I never took them seriously because I didn't think it was possible."

"It was very possible," Vince continued. "The experiments took place right next to where I was held, so I witnessed a lot of them. There were multiple parallel dimensions. That portal was a difficult thing to control. Sometimes, I saw one of them go in there and come out a few minutes later completely beat up. Other times, they would emerge with new information or new technology. The more they went in there, the more they began to change. Both mentally and physically. One day, Okada and Felix went in together, but only Felix came out. No one knew what happened to Okada, and no one dared to ask."

"How long ago did this happen?" Alex asked.

"I can't say for sure," Vince replied and lifted his hands in front of his chest. "I lost track of time after they did this to me."

Alex and Terry exchanged looks of concern.

"I know you two aren't thinking about postponing the mission," Kyle said.

"No. But we have to be very careful." Alex said. "If what Vince is saying is true, then we might be dealing with someone more dangerous than any android."

"That is correct," Vince said. "After the trip where Okada disap-peared, Felix was a completely different person. He stopped visiting his son's facility. He started injecting himself with some sort of green fluid. I don't know what it was, but he never seemed to sleep, rest, or even yawn. He was always on and on top of everything. Our program ramped up quickly after that. That's all I know."

"Why didn't you tell me any of this before?" Terry asked.

"I didn't think you would find the location of the android base," Vince admitted. "It's hidden very well, as you know. The only way for us to get back there is when Felix sends out a homing beacon. Once he turns it off, the location is wiped from our memory."

"What I'm hearing is that we are going into base that's crawling with androids," Kyle said. "They are the new models that kicked the crap out of us at the base; we have to hope that Alex can turn off their server in time, then we have to find Russel and go toe to toe with his Dad, who is known as the Overseer?"

"That's correct," Alex said, looking at Russel through the rearview mirror. "I heard you liked challenges."

"I do, and we are putting an end to all of that," Kyle said. "I've heard everything I need to hear. We can't waste any more time."

"I hate to say it, but I agree with Kyle," Terry said

"Listen up. Here's the plan," Alex said as he prepared to exit the vehicle. "There is no way for us to fight our way through a horde of androids. That's why Vanessa and I will work to shut down the grid that controls the androids and their connection to Felix. Once I do that, you'll be able to infiltrate their base with little opposition. However, you must remain vigilant. There is no do over if this mission fails."

THIRTEEN

T erry took the wheel after Alex exited the car very slowly.

"Good luck to you all," Alex said. "I'll contact you as soon as I do my part."

"And what if-"

"No, what if's Terrance," Alex said. "I've been preparing for this mission for nearly two decades."

"Be careful out there," Terry stuck out his hand.

Alex gave him a firm handshake and gave everyone in the car one last look before he disappeared into the woods.

As he plodded through the uneven terrain, Alex scanned his surroundings to make sure he wasn't being followed. He made his way towards a tree that didn't stand out from the rest of the forest. He stepped on the roots in a specific order and waited for the pin pad to reveal itself. A few seconds later, the tree bark shifted, and the pin pad opened up in its place.

Alex took one last look around and proceeded to punch in a code that very few people knew. Once he was finished, the trees shifted around, and a small shack emerged from the ground. Alex approached the shack with caution even though he knew exactly who was inside.

He opened the door and was greeted by a familiar back of the head.

"Is it time?" the young woman asked without turning around.

"It's time Vanessa," Alex said. He closed the door behind him. "Are you ready?"

"We have the location, thanks to Terry," Vanessa said and spun around in her computer chair. "I'm ready to do my part."

She was also ready to get far away from this shack. It consisted of her computer terminals, a small makeshift kitchen, a bathroom, and a bed. Outside of an occasional trip back to the underground complex, she spent the majority of her time in this place tracking down androids and looking for clues about those who had gone missing over the years. She also hacked as many Coleman Tech systems as she could and looked for those with profiles that would fit their agenda. She was the one who initially found Kyle's profile.

When Vanessa stood up from her chair, she got a better look at Alex. "They really did it to you this time. Are you feeling any better?"

"I will when this mission is completed," Alex said.

Vanessa returned to her keyboard and punched another code before the screen went dark. "My ATV is hidden not too far from here."

"Good," Alex said. "We have to hurry. They'll be in serious trouble if we don't deactivate the server before they get to the Android hub."

Vanessa took a good look at her cabin before heading for the door.

"You did a lot of good work here," Alex remarked as he followed her out.

"I know, but I hope I never have to come back here."

They exited the secret cabin and watched it go back underground as the tree took its place. The rustling of the leaves under their feet added to the sounds of the wildlife that was thriving in this forest, completely unaware of the conflict that was brewing only a few short miles away.

Vanessa climbed the ATV first, and Alex climbed into the backseat a grunt later.

"I presume you know the location," Alex said as he tried his best to get comfortable.

"I do," Vanessa said. She turned on the ATV and pulled up the location on her GPS. "They were right under our noses this whole time, and we didn't know it."

"They were well hidden," Alex said. "Besides, we were always on the defensive. We were worried about our people's safety and remaining hidden. We could have done it years ago if our only purpose was to find their base."

"I suppose you're right," Vanessa said. She made a sharp turn that brought them out of the woods and onto the main road. "Can I ask you something?"

"Sure."

"Let's just say we succeed at taking down the androids. Then what?"

"Then we can help these people regain their lives."

"We've been isolated from the rest of the world for nearly two decades."

"What's your point?"

"We don't know what's out there. What if the rest of the world is just like Reign?"

"I have reason to believe it's not," Alex said cautiously.

"Do you have contact with the outside world?" Vanessa asked.

"Not direct contact," Alex said. "What I have is access to one of the Coleman Tech satellites. I can occasionally pick up news reports or radio transmissions from the surrounding towns. From what I can tell there are no androids and no toxins in those areas. If we can shut down the androids, the boys can shut down the force field, and hopefully, they can get us the formula for the toxin. Then we should be able to reach out to our neighbors for help in dealing with the crisis that's happening here."

"I hope you're right," Vanessa said. "I'd love to get away from this place."

"I'll be staying right here," Alex said with a hint of optimism. "This is my home, and it's going to need me more than ever once we get rid of the android regime."

———

The drive to the newly discovered location meant driving through the center of town in the middle of the night once again.

"Vince has sensors that allow him to detect other androids in the area," Terry said, prompting Vince to join him in the passenger seat.

Kyle remained in the back. He had other things on his mind.

Even though it was the middle of the night, the city seemed more abandoned than usual. Aside from a few leaves blowing in the wind, there was absolutely no movement on the street. No cars, no people, and most importantly, no androids.

"He knows we are coming," Terry said.

"At this point, it doesn't matter," Kyle replied.

"He does know you're coming," Vince confirmed with a blank stare into the distance. "I've tried to block him out. Terry disabled all of the tracking devices that were on me, but there is still a connection between Felix and me."

"That's just great," Kyle said.

"He's been able to acquire technology from multiple dimensions by the sound of it," Terry said. "None of this surprises me."

"You're not the least bit concerned that Felix might know our location now?" Kyle asked.

"If Vince was his way of tracking us, he would have found us six months ago," Terry said.

"You've had this thing for six months?!" Kyle lunged forward as far as he could. Paused. Then looked over at Vince. "I didn't mean to call you a thing."

"It's alright," Vince said, staring into the distance. "I know what I am."

"We're entering the city center," Terry slowed down and turned off the car lights.

They started to reach for their night vision goggles when all of the screens came alive with static.

"This can't be good," Kyle said and looked out of the window.

The static disappeared. It was replaced by a video feed of Felix sitting on his throne with a smug look on his face. "Look at you three trying to sneak through my city."

"What do we do?" Terry asked and looked back at Kyle.

"Keep driving," Kyle said. His eyes were fixed on the screen. "He can't do anything to us through a screen."

"I don't think you understand how much control over this city I have," Felix said and leaned forward. "I don't just control the city itself. I control the people!"

"Just keep driving," Kyle insisted. "Don't listen to this maniac."

"Allow me to demonstrate," Felix leaned back in his chair and looked over at someone off-camera. "Activate emergency wake-up call. Level nine."

"We need to get out of the populated part of the city," Vince said. "Now!"

Terry was about to speed up when a red light emanating from every screen lit up the street, followed by a blaring siren.

"Do you hear that?" Terry asked.

"Sounds like footsteps," Kyle said. "Terry, drive!"

The car began to pick up speed when the doors of every building busted open and the citizens of Reign flooded the streets in a panic.

At first, they ran around aimlessly, grabbing their heads and shaking all over as if the sirens were in their head. Terry drove quickly, with precision, avoiding the people running into the streets.

After a few seconds, the siren's volume decreased, and the people stopped panicking. They looked at each other and then all of their attention shifted to the Jeep.

"They are looking at us!" Kyle said, darting from one side of the car to the other.

Terry kept driving, but it became more difficult as more and more people spilled into the street. "I can't just run these people over!"

"Watch out!" Vince yelled, and Terry stepped on the brakes, forcing the tires to squeal.

There was a boy no older than five standing directly in front of their Jeep.

"We don't have time for this," Kyle said. He pushed the door open, hopped out of the car and ran around to the front. He grabbed the boy and moved him out of the way. "You shouldn't be out anyway. It's past your bedtime."

"Kyle! Get back in the car!" Terry shouted. "They are all coming this way."

Kyle looked up and saw dozens of people heading toward the car from all directions. In a few minutes, half of Reign would surround the jeep.

"Terry, how much further until we get out of the center?" Kyle asked, pacing back and forth.

"Only four blocks, why?"

"Vince, get your big butt out here," Kyle banged on the hood of the car. "Terry, we are going to clear the path. You keep driving."

Vince slammed his door shut and met Kyle at the hood of the car.

"Keep your baton on the lowest possible setting," Kyle instructed. "We don't want to hurt these people. We just need to keep them out of our way. Got it?"

Vince turned on his baton. "I got it."

"Terry," Kyle activated his baton with half a dozen people only a few feet away. "I know we haven't always seen eye to eye. But don't run me over."

Terry shook his head and started driving just as Vince and Kyle began to shove people out of the way as best they could, without seriously injuring anyone.

Felix's face remained on the screen with a proud grin. "Excellent strategy. Making way without hurting anyone. Unfortunately for you, my subjects aren't as compassionate."

The horde paused for a second and looked up at the screen. Felix didn't say anything, but when they turned their heads back towards the car, they all had their mouths open.

"I don't like how they are looking at me," Terry said.

"Oh, you don't like how they are looking at you?" Kyle asked mockingly. "You're inside the car; we are out here!"

"Keep pushing," Vince said. "I know what comes next."

"I don't want to know what comes next," Kyle said and shoved two men out of the way at the same time. As he pushed forward, a woman lunged at him but not with her hands. She attacked with her teeth.

"This is what comes next," Vince said as Kyle jumped out of the way.

"They are biting now?!" Kyle asked. "We need to get out of here quickly!"

Vince and Kyle continued to shove, but the mob became more dense. There was barely any space between the bodies, leaving very little room for pushing. Kyle felt his arms getting tired, and the space around the car began to shrink. If they didn't do something now, the mob would trap them in the middle of town. "Terry! If you have some ideas, this would be the time to share them."

Terry said something from the car but Kyle and Vince couldn't hear him over the noise of the crowd closing in on them. The car came to a stop, and Terry jumped into the back seat and then towards the trunk area.

The mob closed in around the car. Pushing became futile as Vince and Kyle were pushed back toward the doors.

"Grab these!" Terry rolled out the window and handed Kyle two fire extinguishers.

"Vince, catch!" Kyle threw one of the extinguishers over the roof of the car.

Vince caught it with one hand.

They started to spray the crowd around them leaving them no choice but to retreat.

"We have a problem!" Terry yelled out of the driver's side window. "They bit through the two rear tires. I'm losing air fast."

"You got a phone in that car?" Kyle asked.

"Yes, but who can we call?" Terry asked.

"Throw me the phone!" Kyle shouted back, just as the foam from his fire extinguisher started to lose pressure. He caught the phone with his free hand and dialed Wayne. He has two thoughts running through his mind. *I hope I memorized the number correctly, and I hope Wayne picks it up.*

The phone rang three times before a very lively voice picked up. "Hello?"

"Wayne, it's Kyle! I need-"

"Kyle!" Wayne interrupted. "Marshall, it's Kyle. He must be watching the same zombie show we are watching. Remember when I-"

"Wayne!" Kyle shouted into the phone while kicking away a man who wiped the foam out of his face. "If you're close by, I could really use your help!"

"Are you right in the middle of that?" Wayne asked.

"Yes! Are you close?"

"We sure are," Wayne exclaimed. "Marshall, let's take a ride. What do you mean it's not our problem?"

"Get us out of here, and I promise to get you out of Reign by the end of the week," Kyle promised, unable to hide the desperation in his voice.

Kyle heard the clicking sound "Hello! Wayne! Damn it!"

"We are running low on foam," Vince said.

"Yeah, I know Vince," Kyle said, shaking his head.

"What happened?" Terry asked. "Is anyone coming?"

"Doesn't seem like it," Kyle admitted while trying to squeeze out what little foam was left.

A familiar song started playing at the end of the strip that was lined with screens.

Kyle looked up and saw the beat-up ice cream truck rolling towards them. "Terry, it's time to abandon ship. We have to make a run for it."

Terry swung the door open and hit a teenager right in the gut. He shoved him out of the way and joined Vince and Kyle at the front of the parked Jeep. They threw the fire extinguishers at the people closest to them and sprinted towards the ice cream truck.

Wayne slid the door open and stepped back, giving everyone enough space to jump right in. Marshall turned the truck around so fast that it seemed like it was going to flip on its side, but it didn't.

"We are almost there," Vince said. "We just need to get away from the screens."

Marshall slammed his foot on the gas, and the truck sped off away from the screens and the feral crowd.

Kyle looked out of the small round window at the back of the truck and saw Felix's face was gone, and the crowd retreated back towards their homes.

Wayne's eyes darted between Kyle, Terry, and Vince while the three of them sat in silence. Kyle and Terry were trying to catch their breath. Vince sat absolutely still.

Wayne's eyes fixated on Vince. "Kyle, can I speak with you in the front, please?"

Kyle pushed himself up on the floor and stepped between Vince and Terry. Wayne sat down in the passenger's seat and said, "I don't want to start a panic, but I think one of the androids snuck in here with us."

Marshall hit the brakes so hard the whole truck came to a screeching halt sending Terry and Vince tumbling towards the front. They collided with Kyle, who crashed into the dashboard.

"An android is in this truck with us?!" Marshall yelled and reached for the door handle.

Vince stood up first and pulled Terry off of Kyle effortlessly.

"Everyone, relax!" Kyle said, pushing himself off the dashboard. "Vince is with us. He is a reprogrammed android. He helped us get out of that mess back there."

"I said I didn't want to cause any panic," Wayne said quietly while Marshall glared at him.

"We helped you get out of that mess back there," Marshall said and shot Wayne another angry look. "The least you can do is tell us what's happening here."

Kyle gave a brief summary of their mission, along with their destination. Once he was done, Marshall started driving without looking back.

"You're taking us where we need to go then?" Terry asked.

Marshall let out a grunt that was barely audible.

"That sound he just made means we are taking you where you need to go, but Marshall isn't happy about it," Wayne clarified.

———

"We've arrived," Marshall said.

Wayne jumped up and slid the door open. "I hope you guys find what you're looking for in there. If you see a switch that says force field, please shut it off. Thanks."

Kyle looked up at a fairly standard looking, four-story industrial building. He could have passed by it twice a day, and he'd never guess that the forces that had taken over an entire town were operating out of there. "I hate to break it to you Terry, but we are not going to get anything done by sitting in this ice cream truck."

"I know that!" Terry said. "I just need a minute to get ready."

"Okay," Kyle looked back at Vince. "Are you good to go?"

"I'm half machine," Vince reminded everyone. "I was also never exposed to the toxin, so I'm always ready to go."

"Great," Kyle said and stepped out of the truck. "That makes one of us."

Vince and Terry followed Kyle out of the truck and stood off to the side.

"Thanks again for the rescue," Kyle said. "If all goes according to plan, you two will be reunited with your families soon."

Wayne's eyes lit up with hope.

"I'll believe that when I see the shield disappear," Marshall said from inside the truck. "Let's get going, Wayne."

"Good luck in there," Wayne said. "I'd love to help, but this seems to be out of our league."

"I understand," Kyle said.

Wayne climbed back into the truck, and the two men drove away at top speed.

"Vince, you still don't sense any androids in this area?" Kyle asked.

"Nothing outside of the building," Vince said with two fingers at his temple. "I can't sense what's inside."

"This makes perfect sense," Terry added.

"What does?" Kyle asked.

"This building," Terry said with his eyes fixed on the structure in front of them. "This is the Reign water supply center. This is how they were able to spread the toxin to everyone in town."

"That does make sense," Kyle agreed. "It also means that if we get the antidote for it, we can use this same system to spread it to everyone just as they did years ago."

Terry nodded. "We need to get inside first."

"What are we waiting for?" Kyle asked.

Terry shot him a look of annoyance and then placed a small earpiece inside his right ear. "Alex, it's Terry. We've arrived at the site. What is your status?"

———

"We're a few minutes out from the server terminal," Alex said, holding a finger over his earpiece. "Sit tight for now. I'll give you the signal."

Alex and Vanessa had to leave the ATV behind when it became clear that the terminal they were looking for was located in the middle of the densest part of the Reign Forest. The journey was not kind to Alex's injured knee but his armor was designed to help compensate for it.

Vanessa led the way. "We are about five minutes away."

"Good," Alex said optimistically. "When we get there, you do what you have to do. I'll keep watch outside."

"Sounds like a plan," she said and continued the trek through the forest terrain.

The terminal turned out to be a green booth about three feet high with a keypad for a locking mechanism. Just as he had promised, Alex stood watch while Vanessa hacked into the lock to get the door open.

Alex heard the rustling of leaves in the woods and prayed it was only the wind. His prayers went unanswered when he saw three shadows emerging out of the woods.

"Alex, who is out there?" Vanessa asked but continued working on the keypad.

"It's nothing to worry about," Alex said. He grabbed at his utility belt and retrieved a pair of electric batons. "You just focus on the task at hand."

The batons let out a crackling sound as soon as Alex activated them. His eyes were darting between the three shadows until the figures behind them emerged. They were nothing like what Alex had expected. There was no armor, no androids, and nothing that even resembled a human. What came out of the woods was like nothing that Alex or anyone else in his complex had seen before.

They looked like wolves, but their eyes were glowing red. They were covered in black fur, but it wasn't thick enough to hide the metal plates at the top of their heads, shoulders, and backs. The claws and the teeth were metallic as well and reflected the blue electricity that emanated from Alex's batons.

"What are those things?" Vanessa asked in a panic.

"I know it's going to be difficult," Alex said as he bent his knees, preparing for combat. "But I need you to stay focused on what you're doing. I'll handle this."

"There are three of those things!"

"Vanessa!" Alex snapped. "Focus!"

Vanessa's eyes darted back to the keypad. Her lips were trembling, and despite her best efforts, her fingers were shaking as well. She bit down on her bottom lip and resumed her task.

The pack began to close in on Alex. He knew that if he stood around a few seconds longer, they would all lunge at him, and he'd have no chance.

The dog on the left was the closest one to him, so Alex struck it with the baton first, sending it reeling back. The other two jumped on him almost at the same time, but he ducked and struck one of them with the baton as soon as he turned around.

While the other two dogs recovered, the only one that hadn't been touched growled and showed its fangs.

"Well, what are you waiting for?" Alex muttered and brought the two batons directly in front of his chest.

The dog circled around him, looking for an opening, but Alex kept the beast in front of him at all times. When the time came to strike, Alex was so fixated on the dog in front of him that he didn't see one of the other dogs attack him from the side, sending him to the ground. As he went down, Alex made sure to hold on to the baton. He was certain that he stood no chance against these mechanical beasts without his weapons.

Once he hit the floor, he rolled on his side, not giving the dogs a chance to get a hold of him with their jaws. When he got a little room to breathe, he reactivated his baton and struck the two dogs closest to him. This gave him the precious seconds that he needed to get back on his feet.

While he had regained his balance, Alex didn't have any time to catch his breath, unlike his mechanical counterparts, who were right back on their feet, ready to strike. Alex glanced back at Vanessa as the dogs closed in around him.

"I hope you're getting close," Alex called out. "I'm not sure how much longer I can hold them off."

———

"Are you sure you're up for this?" Kyle asked.

"Yes," Terry answered with no hesitation.

"How do we know if Vanessa and Alex succeeded in shutting down the androids?" Kyle asked.

"We won't know until we get inside," Vince replied. "I still can't scan what's inside those walls."

Kyle led the way down a small path that zigzagged between the trees and led up to the front door of the building. Vince and Terry glanced from side to side, expecting an ambush at any moment.

Terry was particularly nervous. He wasn't sure how he was going to react if he was confronted by an android, especially if it was one of the newer models. He knew all of the specs, and the new models had almost no weaknesses. They were faster and stronger than their predecessors, such as Vince, and they were not prone to being paralyzed by jolts of electricity.

At the end of the path, they came across what seemed to be an abandoned lumber yard. There were planks of various shapes and sizes. A lot of them were covered up, and even the ones that were left out in the open didn't show any signs of decay.

The three of them proceeded with caution until they reached the door.

"I'll see if it's open." Kyle stepped up and pulled on the double doors. "It's locked."

"Stand back," Vince said and grabbed one of the double doors and pulled. It didn't budge so he grabbed the handle with both hands and gave it a few tugs until the lock came loose. Vince opened the door slowly and peeked inside. "Everyone get back!"

Vince began to back pedal, but a huge boot emerged from the door and sent Vince flying backwards. An android stepped out and scanned the area.

"It's one of the new models!" Terry yelled.

Kyle looked past the androids and through the door frame. "There are a bunch of them marching this way!"

The android locked his sights on Terry who was pale with fear.

"Terry! Hold him off until Vince recovers!" Kyle ordered and grabbed one of the thicker planks. He dashed towards the door and stuck the plank between the door handles, preventing anyone else from coming through there at least for the time being.

As Kyle ran towards the android, he witnessed Terry unsuccessfully attempting to dodge some punches. This android was a lot faster, and it showed. Kyle picked up the pace and jumped on the android from behind, knocking him off balance momentarily.

Terry, who was bleeding from the mouth, retreated while coughing. Vince ran back into the fray and delivered a strong upper cut to the midsection. The punch had so much force behind it that Kyle felt it while hanging off of the android's neck. He took that as a cue to jump off and joined Vince on the offensive.

The android was blocking all of their attacks with relative ease, even though he was outnumbered. Kyle continued to glance towards the doors where the plank was shaking violently.

Alex and Vanessa had better be close to shutting off that server. We are struggling with one android; we are not going to last long against a dozen, Kyle thought to himself amid the chaos.

"Oh no!" Vince said and stepped away from their adversary. "Not now! Not again!"

"What's wrong?" Kyle asked. The momentary distraction cost him as he got clipped with a punch right in the jaw. He felt like he got hit with a brick and tumbled to the ground.

Vince began to shake his head. He grabbed it with both hands as if to prevent whatever was causing him an immense amount of pain. "I can't have this happen now!"

Kyle stood up and put extra effort into dodging the android's attacks. "Terry! What's wrong with him?"

"I'm not sure," Terry muttered from a distance. He was paralyzed by fear. He knew Kyle needed his help, but he was unable to move a muscle.

"I won't let this stop me!" Vince yelled. He put his hands on his knees and charged at the other android, knocking him down to the ground. He delivered a series of powerful punches that seemed to crush the metal casing of the android's head. "I will not be controlled! You will not stop me!"

It wasn't long before the other android stopped moving. There was smoke coming out of his skull and a black fluid from the corner of his mouth.

Convinced that the threat had been neutralized, Vince stumbled backwards, staring at his hands.

Terry and Kyle approached Vince from different directions.

"Vince," Terry said. "Are you okay?"

Vince grabbed his head once again. "I'll be okay. It's Felix. He is trying to get into my head but I won't let him."

They shifted their attention back to the door. The plank was shaking harder than before.

"How many of them are behind that door?' Kyle asked.

"Dozens," Vince replied. "Maybe even a hundred."

The plank inevitably began to show tiny cracks in the center.

"Kyle! Let's grab another plank!" Terry said.

Kyle didn't move a muscle. "It's no use. I'll never be able to switch it out in time."

"He is right," Vince said. "No plank is going to hold the army that's behind that door."

The cracks in the plank became more visible.

Vanessa, I hope you're working on that server, Kyle thought to himself as he watched the doors. *Another few seconds and this whole mission might be over.*

———

The dogs surrounded Alex just as they had in the beginning. The only difference was that he no longer had the strength to strike first. He stood his ground and prepared to defend himself as best he could. The dogs inched closer as his eyes darted from one to the other. Finally, the dog on his left lunged at him but when he caught it, there was no biting or clawing. The dog was completely limp.

"Got it," Vanessa said with a smile and a sigh of relief.

Alex dropped the dog he was holding and glanced at the other two, laying on their sides motionless. "Are they dead?"

"Not necessarily, but I don't see them coming back online any time soon."

"Okay then." Alex used one arm to lean against a tree and placed the other one on his hip.

"Are you okay?"

"Yes. Thank you. I probably wouldn't have survived a coordinated attack by those dogs."

"You held your own," Vanessa said while putting her tools into her bag. "The stories that I heard about you weren't exaggerations."

"There are stories about me?" Alex asked, genuinely surprised.

"Of course there are," Vanessa said. "You're the leader of an underground resistance group that wouldn't exist without you. Why wouldn't there be stories about you?"

"I'm only doing what needs to be done."

"And yet there was never anyone else."

"I need you to drop me off somewhere before you go off to meet up with the rest of our people," Alex said.

"Let me guess," Vanessa began. "You want to go help Kyle and Terry."

"Yes."

"You need to be checked out by Charlotte. You just fought three cyber dogs or whatever these things are."

"I need to make sure Russel is okay." Alex pushed himself off the tree and staggered forward. "He has been a driving force behind all of the rescue efforts since I went down with the damn knee injury."

Vanessa quickly realized there was no use in arguing further. Alex had his mind made up.

FOURTEEN

The violent shaking stopped abruptly. The door creaked as it seemed like someone was still leaning on it.

Kyle and Vince remained alert while Terry retreated into the background.

"Something isn't right here," Kyle said. He took a few small steps towards the door.

"Wait," Terry said. "I just got a message from Alex. Vanessa was able to shut down the server."

"Good," Kyle straightened up and relaxed a bit. "Vince, help me get this door open. We need to get inside and find Russel."

Terry kept a lookout while Kyle and Vince pushed the door in far enough to remove the pipe that was put in to trap the androids inside. Once they removed the pipe, the door swung open, and six androids fell down on their faces.

"I'm guessing the server shutdown didn't affect you," Kyle said.

"As far as Felix is concerned, I'm an obsolete model," Vince said. "My server was shut down a long time ago. The only reason I'm active today is because of Terry."

Kyle looked back at Terry, who was absolutely terrified. "Let's get inside, Terry. We don't have time to waste."

Kyle was the first one to step over the bodies of the androids and into the building. Vince was right behind him, with a weary Terry a few feet behind them.

They entered into a wide hallway with blue, dimly lit floor tiles and matching ceiling. The walls were white but reflected some of the light that came off the floor and ceiling.

"An interesting color scheme," Kyle said.

"I don't sense any imminent threats in this area," Vince said.

They continued their path down the hall. There were glass doors that wouldn't slide open but none of them seemed to be appropriate places to hold anyone prisoner. The facility was littered with motionless android bodies. Kyle made sure to get a good look at each of them just in case one turned out to be Timmy.

Terry stayed close to the others, but looked back periodically to make sure no one was following him. He had prepared for a day like this for the past two years, but now that it was here, he felt totally out of place. He had sparred with Vince, but he was a much older model. The new androids were designed completely differently. He wasn't sure if Vince would be much help against them if they came across ones that remained active. Terry was convinced that he would be no match for them either. Then there was Kyle, who seemed unphased by the prospect of facing off against androids of any kind. Terry thought it had a lot to do with the fact that he was never exposed to the toxin, as far as he knew, but as time went on, he began to realize that Kyle welcomed a challenge. And there was no bigger challenge than taking down Felix and his army of androids.

They approached an elevator and a staircase at the end of the hall when the blank walls transformed into monitors. They remained blank for a few seconds, with only subtle sounds of static, until Felix's face popped up.

"Welcome to my headquarters," Felix said with a grin. "I don't remember inviting the three of you, but maybe my son did?"

"Where is he, Felix?" Kyle shouted at the monitor closest to him.

"He's up here with me," Felix said calmly. "We are just catching up, but since you insist on crashing our little party, then just take the elevator on your left and meet us on the fourth floor."

The screens went dark.

"We are not taking any elevators here," Kyle said and kicked the staircase door open.

No one protested, and they cautiously entered the staircase. Kyle led the way once again. He kept his back against the wall and looked straight up in case there were any surprises hidden on the top floors. Vince and Terry followed his example until they got to the fourth floor.

When they stepped out into the hallway there were no lit up tiles to be seen. This floor was very basic, with black granite tiles and white walls and ceiling. They proceeded to the end of the hall, where two doors slid open before any of them were even close to them.

Two hands grabbed Kyle by the collar, picked him up, and shoved him back with enough force to send him rolling backward on the floor. He landed at the feet of his two companions. When he looked up, he saw an all too familiar face.

"Timmy," Kyle said while still on the ground. "It's me, Kyle."

"He has no idea who you are," Vince said and helped Kyle off the floor.

"If that's the case, then we are in for a fight," Kyle said.

As the three of them regrouped, the sliding doors opened once again. Two more androids stepped out. They were slightly taller than Timmy, and they wore silver, metallic armor. They sported identical crewcuts but one had red hair while the other one had black hair. They flanked Timmy on opposite sides and began walking forward.

"Vince, what do we know about the newcomers?" Kyle asked as the three of them began retreating towards the back of the room.

"I've never seen them before," Vince said. "They must be new models, which is bad news."

Kyle gritted his teeth. "We are not backing down. We have to get past them to get to Russel."

———

The adrenaline of the fight with the cyborg dogs had worn off almost completely by the time Alex reached the base. He had burning muscles in his legs, and his face was pulsing in too many different areas to count. If he made it to tomorrow morning, his face would almost certainly be covered in bruises.

He approached the base with caution but picked up the pace once he saw a mountain of android bodies at the door. He was relieved to see that Vanessa's code had worked. He was even more relieved not to find the bodies of Terry and Kyle. He didn't know it at the time, but he was walking in their footsteps. He made his ascent up the stairs a lot slower than his allies, but unlike them, he was greeted with an open door to his left. He found it odd but decided to check it out in case there was a threat in there that might sneak up on him later.

He took two steps into the room, and the door behind him slid closed. He didn't turn around. He figured whoever was in control wanted him in this room, and the best thing he could do was to remain aware of his surroundings.

He didn't have to wait long. A bright light turned on and illuminated the far side of the room. There was a man with his face up towards the light as if he was basking in it.

Alex knew exactly who it was the second he laid his eyes on him.

"Hello, old friend," the man said. He opened one eye and looked directly at Alex.

"Felix," Alex said and stepped forward.

"Surprised to see me?"

"Can't say that I am."

"Good. It's only right that you're here. You were there when I started this project, and now you'll be here when I take it to the next level."

"This project? Felix, you've been experimenting on the entire population of this town for over twenty years. This has gone on long enough."

"See, that was always your problem," Felix waved his right index finger. "You were always way too concerned with doing the right thing instead of focusing on the greater good."

"Is this your definition of the greater good? Everyone living in fear?"

"That's one way to look at it. I see it as people living in peace."

"The people of Reign are prisoners of their own minds. No one goes out after dark. No one does any physical activities because they're too afraid to get hurt. No one stands up for what they believe. But that's what you always wanted, isn't it?"

"All I wanted was a place for my son to be safe," Felix said. "And that's what I created. But you had to go and mess with my plans. And now my son doesn't share my vision."

"I gave Russel a choice when I pulled him out of that pod. He chose to do what's right, which is more than I can say for you."

"What you say doesn't matter," Felix said dismissively. "In two hours, I will release a new strain of the toxin, but this one won't affect little old Reign. This one will take over the entire east coast of the United States. This time, there will be no anomalies like yours. No one will know it's coming, and no one will try to stop me."

"No one?" Alex stood up straight, ignoring the pain in his side. His legs no longer ached, and he couldn't feel the pulsing in his face. His heart was beating louder than ever, but he walked up to Felix, and then the two men stood face to face. "What is it you used to say? There are times to take a step back, and there are times to step up. I'm not taking any steps back."

"You think you can stop me?" Felix asked with a smirk. "You've been trying for two decades, and all you have to show for it is that excuse of an underground base and a team of scared brats."

Alex didn't move a muscle. He stood there staring into his former mentor's eyes.

"I see how this is going to go," Felix said. He shed his coat jacket to reveal dark metal armor. "I'm not going to lie to you, Alex. I'm going to enjoy testing out this armor on you."

Alex realized that if he wanted to stand a chance against Felix, he'd have to strike first and he did just that. He cocked back and delivered a strong right fist that was aimed at Felix's face, but two seemingly metal arms were there to block the attack.

Alex felt a sharp pain in his knuckles. He staggered backward and cupped his left hand over his right fist.

Felix circled Alex like a predator stalking its prey. Alex wouldn't take his eyes off him and followed his every move.

"It's a real shame you chose this path." Felix shook his head. "We could have been partners like Okada and I were."

"Were?" Alex asked, hoping to buy himself some time to recover.

"Oh yes. I killed him three years into the project. He got cold feet and didn't want to go all the way down the rabbit hole of the other dimensions."

"You sound absolutely insane," Alex said. "You were messing with other dimensions?"

"Of course I was," Felix replied. "I still am. Where do you think I get all of this new tech from? And why do you think I kidnap all of those kids? It's part of the partnership that I have with them. I send them kids, and in return, they send me their latest technology."

Alex stood up as straight as he could after taking the second beating of the day. "We are going to stop you, Felix. No matter what it takes."

Felix smiled clearly amused. "You were such a nervous young man when you worked for me. That's why you weren't even on my radar once this project picked up speed. But you've been a thorn in my side for years with your moral compass and always wanting to do what's right. Ever since I hired you, it all ends today." Felix marched directly at Alex, dodging his attacks with ease. He grabbed him by the neck with one hand and lifted him up off the floor. "You're not the first one to show up here today with a big plan to stop me."

Alex grunted. He was unable to speak with Felix's hand around his neck. His feet dangled for a few seconds until Felix sent him flying toward the wall behind him. Alex crashed through the wall but luckily landed right on his backside.

"Alex!" Terry shouted.

Alex looked through the dust that came as a result of his crashing through the wall and found Terry, Kyle, and Vince standing behind a red force field.

Alex had never seen such technology. He figured it came from the other dimension that Felix kept talking about. Alex fought to get to his feet. When he was half way up, he saw Felix step through the debris. He looked right past Alex and walked the other way.

"I'll get you out of there," Alex whispered.

"No need for that," Felix was now seated comfortably on his throne with his legs crossed. He had two guards on each side of him. "I'll let them out myself." Felix punched in a code on the arm rest of his throne, and seconds later, the force field was gone.

Kyle rushed everyone to join Alex in the middle of the room. "He's up to something. There is no way he'd release us for no reason."

"You're right about that Kyle," Felix said. He leaned back in his chair and punched another code into the arm rest.

The sliding doors hissed open, and a familiar face entered the room.

Terry let out a premature sigh of relief. "Russel! Thank God you're here!"

Alex placed his arm across Terry's chest, preventing the young man from moving. "Stop. That's not Russel. Look at him closely."

"He's right," Vince said.

"If that's not Russel, then who is that?" Terry asked.

"He has about thirty pounds of muscle under that suit," Kyle pointed out. "I don't care what kind of technology is available here; that's not possible."

They all remained silent for a few moments and analyzed the familiar face dressed in the enemy's armor. The man standing in front of them was indeed bigger. He was dressed in all black with gloves and combat boots. He had a beard that looked like it hadn't been touched in weeks, and he had a blank look plastered across his face.

"You're right to be suspicious," Felix said. "That is not the son that my late wife gave birth to. This is a clone. An enhanced clone at that."

"You cloned and enhanced your own son?" Alex asked.

"You're damn right I did!" Felix said excitedly. "I saw what my son turned into. He was weak, compassionate, and soft!"

"Your son has saved countless lives from your experiments! He's a hero to everyone in my complex." Alex argued, holding on to his right side. He was clearly still in pain from the earlier scuffles.

"Take a look at your hero now, then." Felix punched in another code, and a new set of doors opened up behind the throne. Russel stumbled out. His face was bruised, and his armor was torn all over.

Kyle clenched his teeth and glared at Felix as he ran over and caught Russel before he could collapse to the floor. Felix's enforcers were about to come after Kyle, but he waved them off.

"What happened?" Kyle asked as he helped Russel back towards the rest of their group. "What did he do to you?"

"He exposed me to the toxin," Russel said. "Then I got beat up by…Well… A bigger and stronger version of myself, it seems."

"You did this to your own son?" Alex asked and looked up at Felix.

"That is not my son!" Felix fired back. "He stopped being my son the second you corrupted him with your nonsense! I'm building a new world! And if he doesn't want to be part of it then I have no use for him! Just like I don't have any use for any of you."

Felix pointed at Alex and his group. Timmy and the clone began a slow approach towards their targets.

Alex and Kyle exchanged glances. Terry took a few small steps back.

"This is it," Alex said. He was speaking to everyone, but he was looking directly at Terry. "This is what we trained and prepared for all these years."

"Russel, you stay back for now," Kyle said. He broke away from the group and stepped up towards where the androids were going.

"I'm glad to fight along brave men such as yourselves," Vince said as he joined Kyle in the front. "Even if our chances of survival are slim to none."

"You know some things you can just keep to yourself," Kyle said.

Terry joined them on the front line. He didn't say anything but made eye contact with Kyle, who gave him a quick nod.

Alex was the last one to limp his way towards the front. He put his hand on Terry's shoulder and gave him a soft squeeze.

"Here's the plan," Kyle began. "Vince and I are going to take on my not so little brother over here. Alex, you and Terry are going to take on the imposter. I know you trained the original Russel, and I'm sure the clone shares a few weaknesses even if he is enhanced."

Everyone nodded in agreement as the androids got closer.

"I know now why Russel worked so hard to find you," Alex said, looking ahead at the oncoming threat. "You don't fold under pressure, and you've turned into quite a leader."

Kyle acknowledged the compliment but didn't utter a word. His gaze was fixed on Timmy and the clone, both of whom were moving in sync and at alarming speed.

Kyle engaged Timmy right away, with Vince not far behind.

Alex and Terry let the clone come to them. Alex stood up straight and prepared to defend himself when Terry lunged at the clone and shoved him back. The clone took two steps back, looked up, and attacked Terry with a series of punches and kicks. Terry began to retreat with his hands up. Alex stepped in and broke up the scuffle with a stiff kick to the clone's stomach.

The clone turned his head to Alex, "You're flexible for an old man. Now let's see if you're durable."

Alex put his hands up just in time to absorb a powerful blow from the clone that sent him reeling. Terry saw an opening and jumped back into the fight, not letting the clone gain the upper hand.

A few feet away Kyle and Vince had their hands full with Timmy. Kyle knew Timmy was a more advanced model, but he didn't expect him to overpower Vince and himself so quickly. The fight had only started a few minutes earlier, but they were on the defensive the entire time.

"Timmy! Snap out of it!" Kyle yelled while ducking a punch.

"He can't hear you," Vince said. "He is completely under Felix's control."

Timmy shoved Vince down to the floor which gave Kyle an opening. He crouched down and swept his opponent's feet. Timmy tumbled to the floor.

"Vince!" Kyle shouted, expecting the android to jump on the opportunity while Timmy was down.

Felix stood from his throne and laughed loud enough for everyone to hear.

Kyle knew something had gone wrong.

Vince charged toward Kyle and Timmy, but as he got closer, it became clear that he was coming directly for Kyle. He did his best to defend himself in the few seconds that he had to prepare for this sudden attack. Vince managed to trip him, but Kyle did a backward barrel roll and jumped back up to his feet.

"Vince, what's-"

"You fools," Felix said with a grin on his face. "This android may be an outdated piece of junk, but he is still my piece of junk. I could have taken control of him at any point after you left your precious compound."

The clone had beaten down both Terry and Alex. He picked them up off the floor, slammed them against the wall, and watched them slide down. Once convinced that they were no longer a threat, he joined Vince and Timmy, who were closing in on Kyle.

"Congratulations Kyle," Felix began a slow clap. "You are the last one standing."

"He's not," Russel spoke up. He walked towards Kyle, ripping off the loose pieces of his armor until he was standing shoulder to shoulder with his best friend.

"You've come a long way since I've had to save you from the football team bullies." Kyle ignored the pain in his left shoulder and lifted his arm high enough for a fist bump. "And I'm not going to let you down like I did the last time we teamed up."

"You never let me down," Russel hit Kyle's fist with his own. "I need you to do me a favor. I need you to give me one hundred and ten percent. No holding back."

"You got it." Kyle cracked his knuckles.

"I don't believe it," Felix said. The smirk was now completely gone. "With that amount of toxin, you should be hiding in the corner."

"You should know by now that I never do what I should," Russel said. "That's why you had me cloned. You can control him, but you're not going to control me."

"I've had enough of this!" Felix pointed at Russel and Kyle. "Shut them up!"

The three androids went after their targets, but Russel and Kyle fought back with a renewed sense of confidence. Vince was the first to fall, after Kyle sprayed him with a temporary blinding gas, followed by a hard elbow to the back of the head.

"Sorry buddy," Kyle said as he stood over Vince.

Russel dodged kicks and punches from both Timmy and his clone until Kyle rejoined the fray and put his sleeper hold on Timmy. His arms flailed in the air as he tried to reach back and get Kyle off of him.

"Go to sleep," Kyle said. "When you wake, you won't be under that prick's control anymore."

Timmy passed out a few seconds later, leaving the clone outnumbered.

"You two can't stop me," he said. "I'm the most advanced fighting machine on this planet."

Kyle placed his brother on the floor slowly and was about to make his way towards Russel when he saw him put his hand up and wag his index finger.

"I've got this one," Russel said and shifted his attention to his clone. "Most advanced fighting machine on this planet? Who told you that? Your *Dad* up there?"

"Don't you dare disrespect my father!"

"You don't even know what a father is. I've got news for you. That's definitely not your father; that's not even my father! The man standing up there is probably the result of another twisted experiment."

"How dare you?!" The clone shouted. "I'll shut you up for good!"

Russel cracked a smile, "I'm done running away. Do you think you can take me down again? I want to see you try."

"Arghh!" The clone yelled and attacked Russel wildly. He managed to land a series of punches, but Russel recovered quickly and landed a few punches of his own.

Russel looked back at Alex, who was being helped up by Terry. They both had black and blue eyes and busted lips, but they managed to make it to their feet. Once he regained his balance, Alex unclipped his utility belt and slid it across the floor to Russel.

Russel picked it up without looking away from his clone and strapped it around his waist. He popped open the two pockets closest to his right hip and retrieved a pair of brass knuckles. He tapped them together twice and generated sparks. "This will even the playing field a bit."

Felix descended from his throne, captivated by the confrontation between his son and his clone. Once he was at the bottom of the steps, he quickly charged towards Kyle, who went over to check on Timmy.

"Kyle, watch out!" Alex shouted with the last of his energy.

Kyle turned around in time to see Felix's outstretched arm reaching for his armor. He tried to get away but it was too late. Felix gripped the armor with both hands, picked him up, and sent him flying towards the wall.

Kyle hit the wall with a thud before falling to his knees. He dug his fists into the floor to stop from falling flat on his face.

"This is all your fault!" Felix said, and he stalked Kyle, who pushed himself up off the floor slowly. "You took my son away from me, and now you want to ruin my master plan!"

"Stop using Russel's accident as an excuse to justify what you've done in this town," Kyle said and walked toward Felix. "Your experiment ends today."

"You punk! I'll teach you some respect!"

Kyle and Felix met in the middle of the room and exchanged blows. Felix's blows clearly dealt more damage but Kyle wouldn't stay down. He got up every time and fought back.

"You got lucky with the androids," Felix said. "You're not going to get so lucky with me."

"I never needed luck," Kyle wiped blood off of his forehead before it could reach his eyes. He pretended to throw a punch but pulled back quickly and kicked Felix in the knee. Then he cocked his fist back and punched him right in the jaw, sending the much taller man into retreat for the first time.

Felix recovered quickly and was about to throw another punch when Russel grabbed his arm and shoved him back.

"You?" Felix asked and looked down at the clone who was knocked out on the floor. "How is this possible? He is superior to you in every way!"

"He was made in a test tube," Russel said. He walked over and helped Kyle back to his feet. "It's over. You lost."

"You think this means I lost?" Felix asked and began to laugh uncontrollably.

The android guards approached Felix and stood at his side.

"Looks like he finally lost his mind," Kyle muttered.

"He's up to something, guys!" Terry said as he and Alex joined the others opposite Felix.

"Another genius!" Felix said in the middle of his laugh. He stopped laughing completely and punched a code into his watch. "What happened here represents one percent of the power I truly possess."

Felix took off his watch and tossed it over his shoulder.

"Felix," Alex said. "It's over."

"That's where you're wrong," Felix said and looked back at his watch. "This is only the beginning!"

A bright beam of white light shot up from the watch towards the ceiling. The beam expanded until it was the size of two doors directly behind Felix.

"In a matter of seconds, an army of superior androids from their home dimension will walk through this gateway," Felix said calmly. "And there is nothing you can do about it."

Kyle and the rest of his group took a few steps back.

"Any idea what that is?" Kyle asked. "And how can we stop it?"

"It seems like he still has a component of the watch on his wrist," Terry said. "I'm willing to bet if he goes through that portal, there is a good chance it'll disrupt whatever process he started."

"Any other ideas?" Alex asked.

Terry shook his head.

"Then there is only one thing left to do," Kyle said. "Gentlemen, it's been an honor."

"Wait" Russel said as the reality of what Kyle was about to do dawned on him, but it was too late.

Kyle took off running at full speed towards Felix who was looking back at the portal he had opened. By the time he turned around Kyle had his arms wrapped around his waist. Felix tried to get free but Kyle used all of his strength to pick Felix up off the ground. He used his momentum to push the much larger Felix through the gateway.

"You fool! Let go of me!" Felix yelled as he tried once again to get free and glared at his guards. "Don't just stand there! Help me!"

Terry and Alex used what little strength they had left to intercept the two android guards from getting to Kyle and Felix. The androids wrestled them down with ease, but they were delayed long enough to ensure they wouldn't reach Felix in time to help.

Kyle was relentless. He didn't slow down despite repeated strikes from Felix.

The two of them fell into the gateway together.

As soon as they were gone, the gateway turned back into a beam of light that disappeared into the watch. The two remaining android guards fell lifeless where the portal had closed.

"Kyle!!! No!" Russel ran to where the watch was and snatched it up off the ground. "Terry, quick! Help me turn this thing on!"

Terry limped over and examined the watch. "I'm sorry, Russel. It's dead."

Russel fell to his knees and punched the floor with his right fist. "This can't be. He can't be gone."

Alex put his hand on Russel's shoulder. "We'll find a way to get him back. I promise."

FIFTEEN

Russel pulled the doors shut and held on to them until Alex activated the locking mechanism. The lock screen on the side of the door turned red. Russel let go of the doors and stared at the red light.

Alex walked over with a tablet in one hand and a cane in the other. "Are you alright?"

Russel turned around and faced Alex. "We should burn this place down."

"This town has been through enough," Alex said. "Burning down the main source of clean water would add to a long list of things that we still need to fix around here."

"You're right," Russel said and dragged his feet towards the jeep that was parked at the foot of the hill.

Alex followed behind him at a much slower pace.

It had been almost a month since their showdown with Felix. In that time, they had developed an antidote to the substance that Felix used to keep the city under his control. They used the files stored in the facility's computers and the same water supply system that Felix did all those years ago, to accomplish their mission.

Reign didn't come alive overnight, but little by little, people began to realize that they had been living in a fog for two decades. They needed help readjusting to normal life. Alex and his team had a plan in place to help people, and they did just that.

They held presentations in public places explaining what had taken place in Reign and how things were going to improve. Charlotte put together a team of therapists to help people process what had happened to them, while Terry and Vanessa helped the Reign School Board put together a curriculum that would allow the children of Reign rejoin society.

Russel helped Alex climb into the jeep and then made his way to the driver's seat.

"Don't forget we are going to the fall festival," Alex said as he put his seatbelt on.

"I'm not in the mood for a festival," Russel said and reversed onto the road. "I'll just drop you off and head to the complex."

"And do what?"

"Not sure."

"You need to stop this."

"Stop what?"

"Beating yourself up over what happened."

Russel kept his eyes fixed on the road.

"I had all of the equipment from Felix's throne room transferred to Terry's lab," Alex said. "Now that we are done distributing the antidote, we are going to focus on finding exactly where that portal took Kyle and your dad."

"Terry can't even turn that thing on," Russel said.

"Don't underestimate Terry," Alex said. "He is going to find a way. Now slow down, and make this right."

Russel made the turn and pulled into a busy parking lot. People were streaming out of the parking lot and into the field ahead. Russel took the first available spot and helped Alex out of the car.

The smell of barbeque had traveled to the lot, and Russel couldn't help but crack a smile.

"Smells good, doesn't it?" Alex asked.

Russel nodded.

"Let's go," Alex said. "Charlotte isn't going to be happy if we miss the opening ceremony."

Russel walked alongside Alex who had joined the crowd of people all heading in the same direction.

For the first time in a long time, there was no rescue mission, no supply run, there was only the fall festival to attend. It was an unfamiliar feeling for Russel, but he told himself that he would make an effort to enjoy it.

But only for tonight.

The mission to find Kyle would begin tomorrow, and he wouldn't stop until Kyle was home.

———

Kyle felt a light kick to his stomach. It was followed by a slightly harder and more impatient kick.

"Wake up Mr. Hero," said a familiar voice. "Nap time is over."

Kyle was lying face down on a damp surface. He pushed himself up on all fours and looked over to who was responsible for waking him up.

It was dark outside but there was no mistaking the person who was standing over him.

Kyle felt a surge of adrenaline and jumped up off the floor.

"Relax," Felix said and took a few steps back with his hands up by his shoulders. "I'm not going to fight you."

"What's going on here? Where are we?" Kyle asked. He brushed some dirt off his face but made sure not to take his eyes off of Felix.

"We are in another dimension thanks to your antics," Felix said and looked around. "I'm not sure exactly which one."

Kyle forced himself to look away from Felix and scanned their surroundings.

They were on a plain with grass of different lengths all around them. There were no trees but there was a mountain a couple of miles behind Felix.

"You know where we are," Kyle said. "The last thing I remember was you opening that portal."

"Quiet!" Felix said. "There is something moving in the grass behind you."

Kyle turned his neck and spotted six pairs of bright yellow eyes. He didn't want to turn his back on Felix, but he also didn't want to get attacked by whatever was back there.

"Walk to me," Felix said. "Slowly."

Kyle stepped lightly and made as little noise as possible until he reached Felix. He turned around and stood side by side with the enemy.

"I don't know where we are," Felix whispered. "And I don't know what those things are, but I suggest we stick together until we figure it out."

Kyle gritted his teeth. "Fine."

The owners of the yellow eyes stepped out of the tall grass. They were clearly a pack of wild beasts that were like nothing either one of them had seen before. Aside from the piercing eyes, all Kyle could focus on were the muscular legs and long, sharp fangs.

"Our best bet is to make a run for those mountains behind us," Kyle whispered.

"Agreed. Run!"

-THE END-

FROM THE AUTHOR

Thank you for reading Stolen Ring Time. I hope you enjoyed it and if you did, I'd really appreciate if you'd consider leaving a review on Amazon. New independent authors depend on reviews to make our book more visible to other readers.

If you would like to share your thoughts on the book with me or ask me questions, feel free to email me at yankalandarov@gmail.com. I reply to every email.